The Rise of a King

By: Lewis D McDonald

<u>**Thank you**</u> for giving this tale of mine a read. This is a bridge story between *The Plague of Kavronax* and *The Death of the Shroud*. These stories are independent of one another, but they are all related.

    If you enjoy this story and are interested in reading more, please give any of the other books I have written a try! I love to hear feedback, whether good or bad, so shoot me a message on any of the socials if you'd like.

The Territorial War Series:
Territorial War - The Legends of Old (prequel)
Territorial War - The Birth of Evil (prequel)
Territorial War - (Book 1)
Territorial War - A Battle on Two Fronts (Book 2)
Territorial War - The End of an Era (Book 3)
Territorial War - A Fight for Survival (Book 4)

The Lands of War Collection:
The Plague of Kavronax
The Rise of a King
The Death of the Shroud
The Battle of Fates

The Forgotten Tale Series:
The Forgotten Tale - The Road to Hell (prequel)
The Forgotten Tale - The Island of Cirantha (Book 1)
The Forgotten Tale - For the Good of the People (Book 2)
The Forgotten Tale - Beneath a Perilous Veil (Book 3)
The Forgotten Tale - A Tragedy in Pasea (Book 4)
The Forgotten Tale - Dancing with the Devil (Book 5)
The Forgotten Tale - The Truth Unfolds (Book 6)
The Forgotten Tale - The Death of a Fiend (Book 7)

Follow the series on Social Media at:

Instagram - **@territorial_war**
Facebook - **https://www.facebook.com/TerritorialWar**
TikTok - **@territorial_war**

If you enjoy the story, please leave a review and spread the word!

Pronunciation Guide

Some of the words in this book might be a little out of the ordinary. Refer back to this guide if you need to see how any of the words are pronounced when you see them!

People
Aliyah = uh-LEE-uh
Aslan = OZ-lahn
Dagda = DOG-duh
Daibhal = DIE-ball
Damon = DAY-mun
Dante = DAWN-tay
Faetu = FAY-too
Kinomaru = KEY-no-mah-ru
Kyojin = KEY-oh-jin

GOLDWATER
CRYSTALUNE
SASTILLE
DAWNBERRY
TILLIVILLE
ANGRON PRISON
ANGELWOOD
JAGGED
HUSKBERG
N
W
E
S
BLACKHOLD
GREENFELL

Red Raven Stronghold
Evorim
Roosenhem
Timiston
Unterberg
Acelin
Peaks
Osterfeld
Dondugara
Borsun
Coal Town
Resonation cave

Preface

Large-scale battles have a lot of moving parts and it can be difficult to organize and describe the actions of an individual in a moment of time when many individuals are involved. To help provide more clarity, in this book you are going to see breaks in the fight like this:

~   ~   ~   ~   ~   ~   ~   ~

This break indicates the perspective shifting from one area of the battle to another. This makes it easier to describe what each individual(s) may be doing at a moment in time without creating a confusing paragraph that jumps between too many people and dilutes the perspective.

Multiple moments will be happening within the same period, and breaking the battles up in this fashion will help describe these moments with more clarity. I hope this helps!

Introduction

The lands of Tahlav are in peril under the rule of a vicious tyrant. King Damon has recently seized the throne and begun expanding his Kingdom through blood and violence. Towns on the outskirts of his Kingdom have begun to submit before he arrives to avoid getting their people slaughtered. The chokehold King Damon has on the world around him is only growing tighter as his influence spreads.

Rival Kingdoms have begun to recognize King Damon as a threat, but they underestimate his power regularly, and many Kingdoms have fallen entirely for this mistake. Since his violent coronation as King, Damon has expanded his borders tenfold, consuming rival nations and leaving a sea of blood and bodies in his wake.

Many people have tried to assassinate the vicious dictator, but all of them have failed. His power is too great, and his ruthlessness is a deterrent to any potential threat. No matter what would-be assassins throw his way, he always finds them before they find him, adding to the failed attempts and creating an even more prominent deterrent against future attempts.

Some people have questioned where he originally came from and how he became King, but his origins are shrouded in mystery to almost everyone. The Kingdom he took command of was small before he arrived, so the history is clouded and veiled. But one thing is certain: everyone knows the throne was taken by force, and King Damon will not stop until every inch of the world belongs to him.

Chapter 1

Smoke filled the air throughout the village, carrying ash from burning rooftops high into the sky. The ash and smoke blotted out the moonlight, leaving only the dancing flames to illuminate the area. The fires blazed as they jumped from building to building, slowly spreading their path of destruction.

The tortured screams of dying souls pierced through the constant hum of crackling flames. The smell of burning flesh twisted into the thick smoke and filled the noses of everyone around. The experience was haunting, especially for those too young to understand what was going on.

A young boy named Dante sat in a cellar with two of his friends. A girl named Aliyah and another boy named Faetu. The three of them were hiding beneath Faetu's home, hoping to escape the horrors that were taking place outside, but the smoke was beginning to thicken in the cellar, and they understood that staying there too much longer could mean they would die. They were only ten years old, but they were smart enough to know they weren't safe there anymore.

"Come on, guys, we have to get out of here," Faetu said as he ushered the others to follow him.

"I'm scared," Dante replied with a shaky voice. "It's not safe out there."

"I know, but if we stay here, the smoke will kill us," Faetu argued.

"What about your mom and dad? Are they upstairs?" Aliyah asked.

Faetu's expression shifted as she spoke, letting her know he assumed they were likely already dead. He hesitated before trying to speak, but Aliyah recognized what was going on and quickly interrupted before he was forced to answer.

"I'm with you, Faetu," Aliyah said as she grabbed his arm to try to comfort him.

"Follow me, maybe we can run across the street and hide in old man Crawford's cellar," Faetu instructed.

"Okay, lead the way," Dante hesitantly agreed through a strained cough.

Faetu opened the cellar door to his home, letting a stream of smoke pour from the passageway as the cloud rushed to escape into the air above. The three of them stepped from the cellar, doing their best to cover their coughing until they could gather themselves and decide where to go.

As they stepped outside, the grim reality of what was happening was in full display. Bodies littered the streets, blood stained the grass, and flames consumed everything they touched. It was a scene pulled from a nightmare.

Faetu looked across the street and saw all the houses were already burning before he said, "We'll have to find somewhere else. Stay close, and we'll get out of here."

Dante nodded in agreement, and Aliyah grabbed his arm tightly as they started to make their way toward the edge of town slowly. They stayed as low as they could and stuck as close to buildings as the heat would allow them, hoping to avoid getting seen, but it didn't take long before they stumbled into some armed knights standing behind four men who were on their knees and had their hands tied behind their backs.

The kids quickly ducked back out of sight before they were seen and peeked around the corner to try to figure out what was going on. The knights were standing there, immobile, like gargoyles perched on a ledge. The men who were bound were bruised but alive. However, no one was talking.

"Wait," Dante whispered as he looked at the men, "That's Father Edward."

"Hush, Dante," Faetu said as he pressed his finger to his lip. "We have to stay quiet; there's nothing we can do to help."

"But he's bleeding," Dante insisted.

"Don't worry," Aliyah assured. "Once they leave, I can patch up his scrapes. I'll use my magic."

Dante paused and thought to himself, "Aliyah does have pretty good healing powers, and Father Edward doesn't look to be in bad shape. If we just lie low, maybe everything will be okay. Aliyah has always been adept with her powers, even when we were little, so I know she can take care of him."

"You can rest your mind, Dante," Faetu said calmly. "We will get out of this."

Dante looked at Faetu and continued to think to himself, "And Faetu is always so calm, no matter what the situation is. He always seems to keep a level head and even goes out of his way to calm me down, too. Why? Why can't I be as calm and collected as these two are?"

Finally, Dante spoke aloud, "Okay, thank you guys."

"No need to thank me," Faetu said, "I'll always have your back."

Before Dante could respond, they felt a powerful presence begin to bear down on them as footsteps rang out and seemed to echo off the walls. They couldn't explain it, but it felt as if the air itself had suddenly grown heavier, and an anxious feeling seemed to seize their bodies, making them incredibly nervous.

"What is going on?" Aliyah asked with a shaky voice.

"I don't know," Faetu answered.

Suddenly, a voice rang out, sending a chill down their spines: "Mister Hendrickson, it is a shame this is how we meet for only the second time."

A man emerged from the smoke, dressed in minimal armor, but his gear was pristinely maintained, making it clear he was incredibly wealthy. He wielded a pristine sword that looked as though it had a faint glow along the edge of the blade, but that glow was splattered with blood. He continued to approach the four men on the ground with his weapon in hand and a devilish grin on his face.

"You're a monster," one of the bound men responded.

In the blink of an eye, the nobleman slashed his blade into the neck of the man who spoke, barely touching the tip of his throat. However, the attack still managed to completely sever his head, sending it rolling across the ground as his body fell to the cobblestone and began to bleed out.

"You really should teach your men to hold their tongue in front of their King, mister Hendrickson," the man stated.

"Why?" Hendrickson answered as he stared at the ground in front of him. "Why have you done this, Damon?"

"That is King Damon, and you will address me as nothing else," Damon demanded.

"You are not my King," Hendrickson grunted.

"I wasn't giving you the choice," Damon growled as he slammed his blade into another of the bound men's throats, severing his head just as he did the other.

"Please stop this!" Hendrickson shouted. "It's me who slighted you, so why don't you kill me?"

"It's simple, really. You are the leader of Dawnberry, a quiet and peaceful town at the very fringes of my Kingdom. And as a leader, you are responsible for keeping your people in line. If I killed you, there would be another to take your place that I would have to teach a lesson to.
However, if I slowly killed everyone around you, the lesson would be all yours to learn. Then I don't need to teach anyone else, and the lessons you've learned will then be passed down to those beneath you," Damon explained. "Consider it an investment in Dawnberry's future."

"You would do all of this because I refused to bow?" Hendrickson asked with tears in his eyes. "What kind of monster are you?"

"I'm the monster that other monsters fear," Damon answered coldly. "Now, how many of your people need to die before you step in line?"

Hendrickson looked around at the destruction to his village and knew it was hopeless to resist. There was no way a small village could withstand the might of an army, and he didn't want to see any more of his people killed. He was riddled with regret for ever defying the tyrant in the first place.

"I submit, King Damon," Hendrickson said as tears fell from his chin. "Please, spare the rest of my people."

"Now, was that so hard?" Damon asked as he took his sword and aimed it at the ground beneath his feet.

He planted the tip of the blade into the stone, and a sudden rush washed outward, rapidly flowing through the entire village until it stretched out beyond its walls. As the wave of energy rolled through the streets, it extinguished every flame it touched, including the torches his men carried. One by one, each fire was put out, and the destruction was immediately stopped in its tracks. A feat seemingly impossible for one man to accomplish.

"You see, I can be a benevolent King," Damon said.

Damon plucked his sword from the ground and slung it out in front of him to remove the blood from the blade before he slid it back into its sheath. Hendrickson felt the blood splatter on his face, but ignored it for fear of upsetting King

Damon. However, the priest next to him suddenly fell to the ground with blood pouring from his neck. The blood wasn't from Damon's blade; the King had killed Father Edward.

"Let that be your final warning. If you ever disrespect me, defy my rule, or breathe a singular word of insolence. I will burn this village to the ground and plant the banner of my Kingdom in its ashes," Damon warned.

"NOOOO!" Dante shouted as he peeked around the corner and saw Father Edward bleeding on the ground.

"Dante! NO!" Faetu shouted as he tried to stop him from running around the corner.

Dante quickly tried to scramble to his feet and run toward Father Edward, but Faetu grabbed one of his ankles and tripped him to the ground. Faetu then jumped on top of Dante and planted a knee in his lower back, and then grabbed the back of his head to force it into the dirt.

"What do we have here?" Damon asked as he walked over toward the children.

"Please forgive him," Faetu said as he shoved Dante's head into the ground and bowed his own. "Father Edward has been his caretaker since birth. His emotions have understandably overcome him."

"I will decide what is understandable, boy," Damon barked.

"Yes, sir," Faetu said, keeping his head low.

Dante was furious and couldn't understand why Faetu was so willing to bow to such an evil man. He struggled to get out from underneath his friend's grasp, but Faetu was too strong. As he struggled, he felt a drop fall onto the side of his face. He peeked out of the corner of his eye and could barely see Faetu, but it was enough to tell that tears were falling from his face, and rage filled his eyes. At that moment, Dante understood Faetu was trying to protect him, so he stopped fighting and began to sob quietly.

"If I hadn't already cleansed my blade, I would leave a reminder on the boy's body to remember my mercy, but I have no desire to sully my weapon with any more of the blood of such filth. Let this moment be a lesson to you, child. Those who resist me are sure to burn in flames and bleed like the vermin they are. It would be wise for you to carry this lesson with you until the day that I die and not a moment sooner. Do you understand?" Damon preached.

Dante was quiet; he was filled with anger and hatred and had no desire to answer the call of such an evil person. But Damon was not relenting. He bent down next to the boys, shoved Faetu off of Dante, and grabbed him by the hair to lift him off the ground.

"I'm not sure you heard me properly, but I asked you a question. Do you understand?" Damon said.

Dante looked him in the eyes and was writhing with anger as he thought, "If I grab his sword, maybe I can kill him. I know Faetu can use fire; maybe he and I together can kill him before he gets a chance to move. Yeah, and then Aliyah can patch any scratches we'll get." Despite his idea, he knew better than to try. He knew he couldn't do anything, so he grit his teeth as he answered, "Yes."

"Yes, what?" Damon persisted.

"Yes… Your Highness," Dante responded.

"Good," Damon said as he shoved Dante's head back into the ground. "If you lift your worthless head from this earth before my men and I walk away, I'll cut it off."

Dante said nothing; he just pressed his head into the ground and felt the tears well up in his eyes as he listened to the footsteps slowly fade away into the distance. He heard people moving around, but he didn't budge an inch. He was worried that one of them might still be nearby, and he didn't want to risk getting his head cut off. Damon put a fear into his mind that was unshakeable, and that fear was something he wouldn't soon forget.

After some time passed, Faetu walked over and gently placed his hand on Dante's back, saying, "Come on, they're gone now, you can get up."

Dante slowly pushed himself up, brushed the dirt off his forehead, and sat back on his feet, but he felt no better. The man who had raised him since birth was gone, and he was humiliated by the man who killed him. Dante looked at Faetu and Aliyah. He could see they were hurting as well, but he didn't say anything. He just hung his head and stared at the ground as he tried to process everything.

"We're going to look around and see if we can find any survivors. It looks like most of the damage was to our buildings, not to our people, so we are going to help where we can. Do you want to join us?" Faetu asked.

"Yeah," Dante answered plainly as he looked up at Father Edward.

"I'm sorry about what happened," Faetu said. "It was unfair what he did to Father Edward, and you, too. We'll get him back someday."

Dante looked at Faetu and could see the conviction in his eyes. He meant what he said, even if he was just a kid. He couldn't explain it, but he felt compelled to believe Faetu, and that belief made him feel just a tiny bit better.

"Maybe one day we will get some revenge," Dante thought to himself, "But that day isn't today, or tomorrow. But maybe when we're older and stronger. Who knows, maybe I'll be as strong as Faetu someday."

Faetu stuck out his hand and helped Dante to his feet. He smiled at him and gave him a gentle pat on the back, saying, "We'll get through this together, Dante. Don't worry."

"I believe you," Dante replied.

"Let's go find people who need help," Aliyah urged.

"Yes, and we'll use your powers to help them," Faetu agreed.

Faetu led the others through the village, looking for anyone and everyone they could find. They grabbed any survivors they came across, and Aliyah used her limited magic to heal as many of the wounds as she could. Even at her age, she was surprisingly adept at healing, but her power was limited, and the best she was able to do was patch up the minor wounds. Anyone with severe injuries would require attention from an actual doctor.

Despite the incredible damage to the village, the fires mainly tore through roofs and burned only a small number of houses to the ground. Many of the buildings appeared salvageable with some repairs, which was a good sign.

As for the death toll, it was higher than they anticipated. Nearly a quarter of the village's population perished in the raid. Men, women, and children were among the deceased. No mercy was spared for anyone, further adding to the ruthlessness of Damon's army and the hatred the people had for him. But that hatred was far overshadowed by fear, and after this night, none of the village leaders ever planned on crossing him again.

Faetu eventually made it back to his home to find it was burned nearly to the ground. He hadn't seen his parents since the army left, and in the bottom of his gut, he knew why. As the three children stood outside his home, Faetu prepared to walk inside when Hendrickson stopped him.

"Don't go in there," Hendrickson said. "There's nothing your young eyes should witness within those walls."

"I need to know for sure," Faetu stated.

"No, I've been inside. I can assure you," Hendrickson pleaded. "I am so sorry for your loss, young Faetu, but your parents have passed on from this wretched world."

Faetu stood still with his fists clenched, but his face was blank. He slowly closed his eyes and took a deep breath through his nose, and then slowly released it to calm himself. He then nodded and looked back up at Hendrickson.

"You can stay with me if you'd like," Hendrickson offered. "Both of you can."

"Let's keep looking for survivors," Faetu stated, doing his best to ignore the pain in his stomach.

"Yeah, let's do that," Dante agreed, trying to return the same comfort his friend showed him.

The kids walked away to keep looking for ways to help. They were driven less by the need to help and more by the desire to distract themselves from their loss. Dante was struggling to cope with what happened, but Faetu seemed like his loss only fueled his determination.

The night was tragic for everyone involved, and the events that occurred would haunt them for the rest of their lives. But they had to live on, rebuild, and make the best of their situation. This was the new reality that they were forced to live in, and they had no choice but to push onward.

1
2
3
4

Chapter 2 - 15 Years Later

"Do you ever have nightmares, Dante?" Faetu asked as Dante suddenly sat up with his eyes wide.

Dante looked around for a moment but calmed himself quickly. He rubbed the sleep from his eyes and then looked outside to see that the sun was beginning to rise in the distance. He saw Faetu sitting at the edge of his bed with all of his guard equipment on, so he knew he had been up all night.

The sunlight beamed through the window and lit up Faetu's skin, as if he were the focal point of the room. The light highlighted his strong jaw and handsome features, but his expression was a look of slight concern. Dante shook his head, knowing he probably sat in that spot on purpose.

"Why do you ask?" Dante said as he tried to wake himself up.

"You were mumbling and jerking a lot in your sleep," Faetu answered.

Dante let out a sigh before saying, "Yeah, sometimes."

"Me too," Faetu said with a short laugh as he stared at the ground beneath his feet. "What are yours about?"

"I don't know, different things," Dante answered. "Sometimes it's monsters destroying the village, sometimes I'm falling… and sometimes it's Damon."

"I'm pretty sure he haunts all of our nightmares," Faetu added.

"What about you?" Dante asked.

"Mine is the same thing every time. You are in it as well," Faetu answered.

"What? Are we all being slaughtered by some great evil?" Dante asked.

"No," Faetu said with a blank expression on his face, as if he were lost in thought.

"Then what is it?" Dante asked.

"You, Hendrickson, Kinomaru, Aslan, and even Aliyah are all a part of a large group filled with people I know and care about. Except you are the ones trying to kill me. You all grab at my body, taking pieces from me until I have nothing left, then you leave me in the dirt to bleed and die," Faetu explained. His expression shifted back to a typical cheerful one before he said, "But thankfully, those are just dreams."

"Well, you never have to worry about me taking a piece of your body," Dante dismissed with a laugh. "Aslan, maybe. You're probably safe from Kinomaru, too."

"Speaking of Kinomaru, you guys are up on the next watch shift. I've been up most of the night, so I'm ready to rest my eyes for a moment. That's why I'm waking you up," Faetu explained.

"Right, go ahead and hit the hay, I'll take it from here," Dante said as he gave Faetu a pat on the back and jumped to his feet.

"Okay, don't go back to sleep on me, I heard about the last time for weeks before Hendrickson finally cooled off," Faetu urged.

"Don't worry, I'll make sure not to fall back asleep," Dante assured, "Now get out of here so I can get ready."

Faetu stood while chuckling and said, "The shy type I see. I'll see myself out, wouldn't want you blushing."

"Just get out," Dante said as he pushed Faetu toward the door and laughed along with him. "I'll send someone back around lunch time to wake you."

"And not a minute sooner," Faetu said as he walked out of the door and closed it behind him."

Dante threw on his gear and gathered his things as he prepared for the day. There were many layers to his uniform, and it was always a frustrating experience to put it on, but he knew it was necessary. His hair was long, dark, and thinner than most, so he tied it behind his head to keep it out of his eyes while he got ready.

"Whose bright idea was it to join the village guard?" Dante thought to himself. "We're nothing but a group of misfits anyway. A mute, a thief, a healer, a pyromaniac, and then me, the powerless weakling. I guess our strange dynamic alone is enough to keep threats at bay."

Dante continued to lose himself in thought as he tightened his straps and secured his gear. Once he finished, he stepped out of his door and started making his way toward the guard house to assume his post.

The sun shone brightly on a peaceful day in Dawnberry. The village was as busy as usual, with farmers tending the fields, merchants running their shops, and the rest of the villagers going about their daily lives.

"Another beautiful day," Dante thought. "Dawnberry really has come a long way since I was a kid. I never would have guessed we could have rebuilt, let alone grown in numbers, after what happened."

Dante continued to weave through the streets until the guardhouse was in view. He could see plenty of faces he knew moving around within, so he started to move more quickly to avoid being any later than he already was.

"I'm always running behind. I have to start getting better at waking up on time," Dante grumbled.

He quickly moved through the door and found Kinomaru standing to the side, waiting. Kinomaru was a tall and heavy man, shaped nearly like a bipedal bear. However, atop his intimidatingly large frame sat one of the most welcoming faces to ever grace Dawnberry. Dante walked over, patted his friend on the arm, and motioned for the door.

"Sorry I'm late, big guy," Dante said as he waved Kinomaru onward, "Let's get out of here."

Kinomaru nodded his head in agreement and followed Dante out of the building. They then started their patrol around the edges of Dawnberry to make sure nothing troublesome was happening.

They walked quietly, not saying a word to one another, enjoying the peaceful, cool breeze and warm sunlight that took their turns dancing on their skin. The day was as beautiful as any other, and Dante's mind wandered as it always did.

"You know, I think I may finally come out and say it, Kinomaru," Dante said as they walked.

Kinomaru looked down at Dante, an eyebrow raised, but he didn't say anything; he just waited for Dante to continue instead.

"I think I may finally tell Aliyah how I feel about her. I mean, we've known each other for so long now, so I know I shouldn't be nervous. But I've always been scared to tell her," Dante continued.

Kinomaru continued to listen to his friend, but didn't say anything in response.

"But, I know she loves Faetu," Dante said with a sigh. "And he is too difficult to read, so I don't even know if he feels the same about her. I mean, it's not like they're betrothed, so I could still profess my feelings. What do you think?"

Dante looked over at Kinomaru, who was actively listening, but his expression was blank. It was clear he was actively engaged in the conversation, but his emotions or responses were almost impossible to read at times.

"Right, you don't talk. I don't know how I could have forgotten," Dante said sarcastically. "You know, you've been here for years, why don't you talk? Do you not understand what I'm saying, or have you taken some sort of vow of silence?"

Kinomaru remained silent, but he gently smiled at Dante, which was oddly comforting.

"Actually, I kind of like the fact you don't speak. It means I can confide in someone without worrying about my secrets being spilled. I appreciate that," Dante praised.

Kinomaru placed his hand on Dante's shoulder and gave him a respectful nod, as if to say 'You're welcome'.

"Now, we've done almost two full laps around this place, and I haven't spotted a monster, thief, or damsel in distress one. So, what do you say we find some shade and rest our legs for a moment?" Dante suggested as he turned inward toward the town.

The two of them made their way to a local shop and grabbed some drinks and a quick bite to eat, and then sat down in the shade to rest their legs.

"You know, Kinomaru, you may be the strongest person in the watch," Dante started speaking. "Faetu is pretty strong with his pyrokinetic abilities, but he can't hold a candle to your raw strength. Aslan is probably the closest to you, but that's only because he was professionally trained. He may be able to use his speed to counter your power, but I doubt it would work long enough to win. I guess it doesn't matter in the long run, but know my coin is on you."

Kinomaru heard what he said, but was reactionless as he took a bite of his sandwich. He continued to eat as if nothing was being said to him, ignoring the compliment entirely.

"I'll get him to talk one day," Dante thought to himself.

"How's it going, you two?" A familiarly beautiful voice spoke from behind them.

They snapped around to see Aliyah approaching and grabbing a seat next to them. Dante was immediately flushed and stumbled over what to say.

"W-we're doing good, Aliyah. H-how about you?" Dante stuttered.

"Honestly, just a little bored," Aliyah answered.

"Yeah, me too," Dante agreed.

"Don't get me wrong, I am happy that nothing bad happens here too often, and the worst we deal with is the passing thief or drunk. But part of me wishes for something more exciting. Something that I could truly test the limits of my power," Aliyah explained.

Dante stared at her longingly; he was absorbed into every word she spoke and present for every gesture she made. It was as if she were the only person in front of him, and he was lost in the moments as they passed. He felt like he was riding the waves of her ocean blue eyes as he listened to her speak. Her long, dirty blonde hair flowed over her shoulders, creating something like a frame around her face. Her beauty was a painting Dante could stare at for an eternity.

"I agree with you," Dante replied. "Unfortunately, for you to test your powers, someone else would have to be in pretty bad shape."

"Are you volunteering?" Aliyah teased.

"If you want me to," Dante answered without thinking.

"Huh?" Aliyah asked, confused.

"Uh, I-I mean, if it's bound to happen to any of us, it'll definitely ha-happen to me," Dante replied in a startled tone.

"Maybe I'll just have to follow you around if the fighting starts then," Aliyah joked.

"That would be your best bet," Dante agreed with a nervous laugh. He started to think to himself, "Joke's on her, I would rather enjoy that."

"So, anything exciting happening on your patrol?" Aliyah asked.

"Y'know, I think we saw some border violence between two squirrels, but other than that, no. It's been a relatively peaceful day. What about you? Anything interesting?" Dante asked.

"Not really, just stuck babysitting for the knights," Aliyah answered.

Dante's jaw clenched at the mention of the knights. They were part of the army that worked directly under King Damon, and a haunting reminder of what happened all those years ago.

"They're still around?" Dante asked.

"Yes, sadly. They seem to be excited about something, but they aren't exactly telling me what for," Aliyah answered.

"My guess is they have some poor village to destroy or lives to ruin."

"Those bastards are just as sick as their King," Dante muttered.

"Be careful, you don't want one of them hearing you," Aliyah stated.

"You're right, I'm sorry," Dante said with a nod.

"They should be leaving tomorrow, and then we won't have to worry about them for a while," Aliyah said. "I know everyone is ready for them to leave."

"They don't care," Dante grumbled again. "I'm willing to bet they get their rocks off just by knowing everyone hates them, but no one can do anything about it."

Kinomaru tapped Dante on the chest to get his attention, showing him that a group of knights was walking past. The three of them went silent as the group passed, hoping to avoid any interaction, but it didn't help. The three knights started to approach the group as soon as they spotted them.

"Now, why are three of Dawnberry's finest sitting around in the shade? Shouldn't you be looking for crime to stop?" one of the knights asked with a laugh.

"We've already done our rounds," Dante answered.

"And what does that have to do with anything I'm saying?" the knight asked sharply. "It would be unfortunate if someone were to start a fight, or to steal, or anything else tragic… wouldn't it?"

Dante knew the man was threatening him, and he wanted to say something, but he knew it would spell disaster. He took a deep breath to try to calm himself as he let it out slowly and stood to his feet.

"Come on, Kinomaru, we should check the perimeter," Dante mumbled.

"You really should do that," the knight said with a sinister tone.

Kinomaru stood to his feet, and the knights realized just how large a man he was. This didn't intimidate them; just the opposite, it almost seemed to get them excited. They were itching for a fight and looking for any excuse to start one, so they were exceptionally agitating to everyone around them.

Dante and Kinomaru started to walk away. Dante said his goodbyes to Aliyah before they turned the corner and put some distance between them and the knights. Aliyah returned the gesture and began traveling in the opposite direction.

"Damn those knights," Dante groaned. "I rarely get the chance to talk with Aliyah, and they had to come along and ruin the moment. One day, we will get rid of those bastards and free Dawnberry from their reign if I can help it."

Kinomaru had a slightly furrowed brow as he listened to Dante, but otherwise he was as expressionless as usual, leaving Dante to guess what his response was. Dante continued to complain about the knights for a few more minutes, but eventually he calmed enough to drift back into silence and look around at the scenery. The silence mostly continued until their shift was coming to an end, just before supper.

As the sun was beginning to vanish behind the trees to the west, Dante and Kinomaru made their way toward the pub to get some food. They grabbed a meal and found a table where their friends were sitting, holding a spot to join them.

"I was starting to think that was never going to end," Dante said as he sat in his chair.

"But you had the pinnacle of engaging conversation with you," Aslan laughed.

Kinomaru looked at him briefly before brushing off the comment and focusing back on his dinner.

"It beats having to spend the day with you," Dante joked. "At least it's a peaceful walk with Kinomaru. You're almost as likely to start trouble as you are to solve it."

"Look, it was one time, and I haven't been in hot water since. But you guys won't let me live it down," Aslan said, rolling his eyes.

Aslan was a smaller man, but he was surprisingly agile and adept with his swords. His hair was short and ruffled, and his eyes were a dirty green. He was roguish and off-putting to some, but he was kind at heart.

"I mean, you somehow took a harmless dispute and escalated it into a fist fight. One that you were involved in," Faetu said with a hearty laugh.

"I personally think you've shown you're past that," Aliyah said.

"Thank you," Aslan added. "At least one of you has some sense."

"Yeah, but the rest of us will let you live it down when you're dead," Faetu laughed.

"Eh, you'll never get the chance to see me dead, I'll outlive every single one of you," Aslan boasted.

"We'll see about that," Dante interrupted. "You have a knack for finding yourself in trouble."

"That's only because of all of you," Aslan dismissed. "Anyway, what's our plan for this weekend? All of us have the days free of responsibility. What should we get ourselves into?"

"I can't, guys, I was just assigned to weekend watch this morning, before the end of my shift. Looks like I'll be busy," Faetu sighed.

"What? That's ridiculous," Aslan growled. "We haven't had the proper chance to get into trouble in months."

"Well, with Damon's knights around, we have to be extra vigilant. If we take our eyes off them for a second, they could do something drastic, and we don't want that," Faetu pointed out.

"Has Dawnberry always been like this?" Aslan asked. "I know what happened when King Damon first arrived, but was this place much different before?"

"Yes, quite different," Faetu answered. "We didn't even have a guard put together at all. We were such a small town, we figured it wouldn't help at all if we did. When Damon showed up, we were quickly shown the error of our ways. His people were in the village before anyone even knew."

"So by the time you and Kinomaru arrived, we were already on edge as a people. We never want to suffer another tragedy like that again," Aliyah added.

"You never told me how you ended up here," Aslan said, looking at Kinomaru."

Kinomaru looked back at him and raised an eyebrow, but didn't flinch at the attempt to get him to speak.

"I didn't think that would work," Aslan huffed.

"He showed up here a few years before you did. Unlike you, he was in perfect health. He just strolled in, sat down, and never left. None of us knows his story, and he has never even muttered a single word. But, he is handy with a hammer, and is a perfect fit as a guard," Faetu explained.

"You, on the other hand, showed up covered in blood and running for your life," Dante said with a laugh.

"Yeah, well, I made some poor choices and lost a finger for my efforts," Aslan dismissed. "But I'm still breathing, can't say the same for most of those who were chasing me."

"And now that you all are here, I could never imagine spending my evenings with a different group of fools," Faetu said with a laugh.

"And our group of fools will be missing its ringleader if you can't come with us," Aliyah said as she placed her hand on Faetu's shoulder.

"I will be thinking of you guys while I'm on patrol," Faetu sighed. "But I cannot allow the knights a chance to harm one of our people. Damon has done enough damage here; I won't allow him to do any more.

"I can't stand that man. One day, he's going to get what he deserves," Dante growled.

"And what would that be?!?" A voice shouted from another table.

"Shit..." Dante whispered under his breath as he realized a group of knights was sitting at a table nearby.

"Pardon me?" Faetu said, trying to divert their attention and defuse the situation.

"What might the King deserve?" the knight shouted back as he stood from his table. "And which one of you filthy peasants dares to speak ill of the King?"

The entire pub fell silent as soon as the knight raised his voice. The tension was instantly thick, and the rest of the patrons snapped their attention toward the knights to see what was going on. Everyone knew an attack against the knights spelled certain death, so they were afraid.

Faetu placed his hands up as a show of peace and said, "You must have misheard; none of us spoke ill of King Damon."

"I know what I heard," the knight argued as he walked over to the group. "One day, he's going to get what he deserves. That's what you said. Of course, any filthy peasant like the lot of you would think that."

The knight paused for a moment of silence as he looked around at the group. He took a moment to stare each of them in the eyes, attempting to judge their resolve. He could see they were scared, but also prepared for a fight.

Dante's mind was racing as he thought, "Shit, what do I do? What do I do? Aslan looks ready to reach for his swords at any moment, and Kinomaru seems prepared to jump. If either of them strikes, it will start a massive brawl.

If a fight breaks out, we could probably kill them, right? Shit. But even if we did, it would spell doom for the rest of the village. King Damon would come back here and wipe out everything.

Maybe we could evacuate after we kill them? Damnit, no. There's no way we could relocate the entire village anywhere fast enough, and even if we did, he would find us.

No, I can't have anyone dying because of me. I have to say something. Even if it means I die today, I cannot allow anyone else's death to rest on my conscience."

"I'm not waiting another second. Whoever said that had better come clean right now, or I will have no choice but to punish the entire village," the knight threatened.

Dante immediately started to say something, but he felt a subtle stomp on his toes and heard Faetu speak up before he could react.

"It was me," Faetu stated, still holding his hands up as a sign of surrender.

The knight barely let him finish his sentence before he slammed an uppercut into his stomach, forcing Faetu to keel over from the wind being knocked out of him. Aslan, Aliyah, and Kinomaru immediately started to stand up, but Dante just stared at Faetu with a confused but scared look on his face.

"NO! Stay back! None of you move from your seats," Faetu shouted.

The knight kicked him hard in the ribs as he said, "That's no fair, then my friends don't get a chance to have any fun."

Faetu tried to stand back up on his feet, but the knight kicked him in the side of the head and nearly knocked him unconscious. The knight reached down and grabbed him by the collar of his shirt before lifting him to his feet. He held Faetu steady as the young man tried to maintain his balance.

"Easy, you okay?" the knight asked. "I wouldn't want you passing out on me."

Faetu took a breath and felt the blood pouring from his nose; he could taste it with every swallow. He shook his head and then looked at the knight to respond, but was smashed in the face with a hard overhand punch that sent him stumbling away.

"Why, Faetu?" Dante thought to himself. "Why are you doing this? Why did you lie for me? Ever since we were kids, you have always gone out of your way to protect me, but why? I don't understand."

The knight started to walk Faetu down, crashing a powerful blow with each step he took. A jab to the face, a hook to the ribs, an uppercut to the chin, another hook to the eye, and then a powerful kick to the chest that knocked him onto his back.

"Why am I not moving? I need to help him!" Dante panicked in his own mind. "If someone doesn't step in, Faetu is going to be killed, and it will be my fault."

Dante started hyperventilating, and he could feel his pulse skyrocket. The blood felt like it was coursing through his veins at an incredible pace, circulating through his entire body in a second. He began to feel nauseous, but knew something had to be done. He could see the knight kicking Faetu over and over, and refused to see his friend die. He started to stand but felt like he was going to puke, and before he could, the door to the pub burst open.

"What is going on here?" Hendrickson shouted as he and four armed men started walking toward the knights.

"Your guard here was speaking ill of the King; he needed to be corrected," the knight said with a laugh.

"And did he ever raise a hand to you?" Hendrickson asked.

"No, sadly," the knight answered.

"Then bound by King Damon's law, you have no right to kill him," Hendrickson stated sternly.

"I'll kill whoever I damn well please," the knight threatened.

"And then you will be promptly killed for your transgressions," Hendrickson replied, unwavering.

The knight looked at him for a moment, then down at Faetu, then over at the rest of the group. He could see that pushing it any further would lead to a loss due to the number of people alone, and he could see they were willing to rally behind their leader.

"It's safe to say the boy has learned his lesson," the knight said as he relaxed his stance. He looked over at the other knights and said, "Let's get out of here."

The other knights obliged and started to follow him out of the pub. They laughed as they passed Faetu, as if this were all a big joke to them. They stepped over him disrespectfully and made sure to rub in the damage they had done.

"I didn't think we were going to get any action until we advanced on Blackhold," one of the knights said as they walked away.

As soon as the last knight exited the pub, Aliyah immediately slid down to Faetu's side to start to heal his wounds. Dante slowly walked over to him and knelt next to him as well. He looked at Faetu's bloody face and was dumbfounded to see he was smiling.

"Why are you smiling?" Dante asked quietly.

"What's the matter? You act like you just got beaten up or something," Faetu asked as he looked at Dante.

"I don't understand. Why did you do that?" Dante asked.

"Because, like I've told you before, I always got your back," Faetu said as he playfully punched him in the chest.

"He could have killed you," Aslan said from the table.

"But he didn't," Faetu argued.

"I don't know what the hells happened, but what are you thinking by provoking the knights?" Hendrickson snapped. "Especially the three of you."

"It was my fault, sir," Dante admitted.

"Is that supposed to be better? Look what that led to. You all know the dangers of playing with that particular fire, yet I always find you dancing around it. How far does this need to go before you stop? Does one of you need to die? Does one of us need to die? Or will you not be satisfied until all of Dawnberry is gone?" Hendrickson scolded.

"I'm sorry, sir," Dante stated with his head hung. "It won't happen again."

Hendrickson let out a slow sigh before saying, "Look, I know how you all feel about King Damon, especially you two boys, but you have to move past that. I was hoping all those years growing up alongside Aliyah and her parents would calm the two of you down, but you are just as stubborn now as you were when you were ten."

Aliyah let out a sharp breath as she finished healing some of the swelling and many of the cuts and bruises on Faetu's face. As she caught her breath, she said, "Well, mother did try."

"We'll be alright, sir," Faetu assured. "See, only a few scratches on me, and no one else was hurt. I'll make sure this doesn't happen again."

Hendrickson took another breath to calm himself as he looked at them again. He viewed them as children of his own blood at times, given the role he played in helping raise them, but he worried about their safety. However, he had to place the safety of his village above his own personal feelings, and he knew it.

He shook his head once more before saying, "I can't have you raising any more trouble like this. If an escalation happens between you and the knights again, I will be forced to exile you from Dawnberry to protect everyone else. Please don't make me do that."

"I promise we won't, sir," Faetu agreed. "We'll mind ourselves."

Hendrickson nodded in affirmation and left the pub with the other guards following behind him. Once he was gone, Dante and Aliyah helped Faetu to his feet, and they sat back down at the table. Tension was still incredibly high, and the patrons mainly sat quietly, watching Faetu to see if anything else would happen, but everything slowly began to return to normal.

"I know you're stronger than that guy. Why didn't you beat his ass?" Aslan asked.

"Because that would have spelled doom for the rest of you," Faetu answered.

"That's fair," Aslan digressed.

"I still don't understand," Dante said, "Why did you stand in for me? I should have taken that beating in your place."

"It's no big deal," Faetu dismissed, "Besides, they already don't like you. It would have been a much worse beating if he had the chance to get his hands on you."

"Then I may not have been able to heal it all," Aliyah added.

"So, it all worked out for the better," Faetu continued.

"But still, it's not fair for you to take punishment in my place, Faetu," Dante argued.

"You never asked me to, and I didn't ask if you needed it," Faetu dismissed. "If it makes you feel better, I did it for the safety of all of Dawnberry, not just you."

"Well, thank you, Faetu. I still think someone should do something about this, save the people from Damon's tyranny," Dante said after looking around to make sure no one else was listening.

"Hey guys, I just had a thought," Faetu blurted with a smile from ear to ear.

"What is it?" Aslan asked.

"I think I'm going to ask for this weekend off. I have an idea of something we could do," Faetu answered.

"Fan-tastic," Aslan said with a chuckle. "You're telling me that knight beat some sense into you?"

"Our fearless leader will be joining us after all?" Aliyah said, looking longingly at Faetu.

"I realized that we have to spend some time together; it really has been too long," Faetu laughed. "I'll explain what I have in mind tomorrow, once we've all rested."

"If you say so," Aslan agreed.

"I wish I could be like him," Dante thought to himself as he looked around at everyone. "He effortlessly draws out everyone around him; even Kinomaru is smiling. He's strong, charismatic, and a natural leader. And Aliyah looks at him the way I look at her... I wish I weren't so weak."

"Everything okay, Dante?" Faetu asked.

"Yeah, I'm excited too," Dante answered, snapping himself from his thoughts.

They finished the night with a hearty meal and a drink before turning in. They were looking forward to the weekend, as it had been weeks since they all got out and spent some time away from duty. The minutes ticked by in what felt like seconds, and they parted ways to get some rest.

Chapter 3

The next day, everyone started gathering at the pub for breakfast. Their assignments were uneventful for the day, so there was leniency in where they had to be. They were all talking and laughing as they waited for Faetu to see what he had planned for the weekend.

"I'm telling you, I think that punch would have knocked out Kinomaru," Aslan argued.

"No way," Dante disagreed, "I know Faetu is strong, but he's not stronger than Kinomaru, none of us are. If he can take the punch, so could Kinomaru."

"You know Kinomaru is right here, right?" Aliyah said, pointing at their friend.

"Yeah, but it's not like he's going to argue with us," Aslan noted aloud.

Kinomaru nodded his head slightly, but gave them little more than that.

"So, I will speak on his behalf," Dante answered. "And it would take a lot more than that to put Kinomaru down."

"I think I may have to agree with Dante," Aliyah added. "We've seen just how strong Kinomaru is, even if he is a big softy on the inside."

"What?" Aslan asked, confused.

"Hey, guys," Faetu said as he walked up to the group.

The cuts and bruises on Faetu's face were virtually non-existent. His short blonde hair was free from bloodstains and his skin was free from damage. He carried the same confidence in his posture that he always had. If you weren't there, you would never have known he took a beating the night before. He was as devilishly handsome as always.

"You look better," Aslan said with a playful nudge.

"I was in good hands," Faetu chuckled as he looked over at Aliyah.

"We take care of each other," Aliyah said with a smile.

"So, what were you thinking for this weekend?" Dante asked.

"Are we going to hit the shops and spend a weekend buying things?" Aliyah asked.

"Or are we going to strike out of Dawnberry and travel to a different town to stretch our legs?" Aslan prodded excitedly.

"Or, we could hit the fishing spot Kinomaru likes, it's quite peaceful," Dante suggested.

"We don't need peace, we need adventure," Aslan argued.

"None of the above. No, I think we should kill King Damon," Faetu stated bluntly.

The group's tone shifted immediately. Even Kinomaru's brow furrowed as Faetu mentioned the idea. Dante started to choke on his food and had to cough up a piece of bread.

"That's not the kind of adventure I had in mind," Aslan muttered.

"What?!" Dante asked as he caught his breath.

"You heard me right," Faetu said as his smile faded. "We should kill Damon."

"Are you crazy? How are we supposed to accomplish that?" Aslan asked.

"I've done a lot of thinking, and I had two things jump out at me yesterday. One, we could never lash out for fear of what would happen to the village. But if we attack far outside of the village, it can't be tied to them and won't be their fault. And two, it sounds like the knights are getting sent south, so the war campaign along the southern border is bound to gather Damon's attention. We could probably find the best time to strike while he is busy with the war," Faetu explained.

"Even if the stars aligned and we managed to get him alone, what could we do? We saw how strong he was and what he was capable of doing. How could we ever defeat that?" Dante asked.

"We saw how strong he was fifteen years ago, when we were kids. Our memory is likely making him seem like he was this impossibly powerful man, but we were young, impressionable, and easily frightened. We're not kids anymore, and we are plenty capable. I am certain that our efforts will end in his defeat," Faetu argued.

"What do we have that could combat him?" Aslan asked.

"Our team is the perfect group. Think about it, we have my flames, Aslan's speed, Kinomaru's strength, Aliyah's healing, and..." Faetu paused as he looked at Dante and smirked.

"I know, I'm not as strong as all of you," Dante said as he hung his head.

"I was going to say, and we have Dante's destiny of greatness," Faetu said confidently.

"Huh?" Dante exclaimed, confused.

"You may not see it now, but I know you're the greatest of all of us," Faetu explained.

"I'm not seeing it either," Aslan said sarcastically.

"Me neither," Dante said through nervous laughter.

"Call it intuition, but I know you have greatness within you; it just hasn't been realized yet," Faetu declared.

"Well, I'm glad you feel that way, because I certainly don't," Dante sighed.

"It's true," Faetu said with a wink.

"You don't have to butter me up anymore, I'm in," Dante said, waving off Faetu's comments.

Faetu laughed as he gave Dante a friendly nudge, but his expression shifted back to a serious one before saying, "In reality, what I want to do is not only dangerous, but it would make us outlaws if we get caught or fail. I understand I am asking you all to do something life-changing. But, I believe that you all feel the same way I do, you are ready for life to change. If you want out now, I will never hold a grudge, but once we start this, there is no going back. Is everyone still with me?"

"I'm ready," Dante affirmed.

"I guess I'm in as well," Aslan reluctantly agreed.

"I'll follow wherever you lead," Aliyah claimed.

"And you, big guy?" Faetu asked, looking at Kinomaru, who only cracked him the slightest smile. "I knew you wouldn't let me down."

"But that still doesn't answer how we're going to do this," Dante reminded.

"Today, before the knights leave, we should do some reconnaissance. We can dig for as much information on the battle strategy as possible and come back together with anything we can find. We can meet up at my place. After that, we'll pool together what we've gathered and come up with a solid plan," Faetu explained.

"I'll see what I can dig up. I'm pretty sneaky. I'll lift some things out of some pockets," Aslan said.

"I'm sure I can pull some information out of some men with loose tongues," Aliyah said coyly.

"I'll try to snoop in and see what I can hear," Faetu stated.

"I'm sure I can find something as well," Dante added, "I'll look around all day."

Faetu looked at Kinomaru and said, "You can sit this one out if you want. As for the rest of us, we'll gather everything we can. Let's reconvene at nightfall and pool together what we have."

"Sounds good to me," Aslan said as he stood from his chair, "Best of luck to you guys."

"I'm right behind you," Faetu said, holding up his finger.

"We'll catch up tonight," Aliyah added.

"Best of luck to everyone, and please be careful," Dante urged.

The five of them split ways and went about their separate business. A fire was lit in each of their hearts, giving them the feeling that they could tackle any obstacle. With this newfound sense of determination, they all set off to gather any information they could from the knights in the area.

Dante walked away from breakfast with purpose in his heart. He wasn't sure how, but he was determined to find something useful for everyone before nightfall. He was desperate to return to everyone with some kind of information, because he was tired of feeling like the weakest link.

"Maybe if I follow around one of the knights, I can hear them talk about something important? No, I'm not sneaky enough to get away with that for too long. What if I stole a chest from their caravan? That'll be sure to turn up something important! Unless it's just a chest of gold, then all I'll be doing is bringing attention to myself. Damnit, what can I do?" Dante pondered as he fretted over his options.

He looked around as he paced through the village. He was hoping something would jump out at him that would be the answer to his worries, but he had been having no luck all morning. However, as soon as he turned the corner to the pub, he felt his luck change.

Sitting at an outside table of the pub was the commander of the knights in the region. The commander rarely stepped out of his tent, and an idea popped into his head that he sprang on immediately.

Dante shifted direction quickly and turned for the edge of town, where the knights had their camp established. He made sure to draw as little attention to himself as possible, but started surveying the campsite the moment it was within view. He wanted to soak in as much detail as possible without making it look obvious, so he walked past it until he could slip behind a nearby building.

As soon as he tucked behind the building, he crept to the edge and peeked around to see if anyone was watching for him. He assumed no one had, so he began to observe the camp more closely.

There were guards at the entrance to the camp, but it wasn't surrounded by walls, so it would be easy to get around them. However, a few guards still patrolled the area, so he watched them closely to observe their marching pattern. He knew that getting caught within the encampment would mean he would be executed on sight, so he was diligently watching to make sure he didn't miss any details.

After nearly an hour of watching the different paths the guards walked and where they stopped to communicate, he finally felt like he could see his opening. The grass on the southern side of the camp was exceptionally tall, so he could move in close using it as cover. He sprang into action and wasted no time.

He stepped back out onto the road and walked a little farther south before slipping off the path again and preparing to crawl through to get closer to the camp. The crawl was painstakingly slow, but his movements drew no attention, so his plan was working. After thirty minutes of crawling at a painstakingly slow pace, he finally reached the very edge of the camp. He could barely see people walking around within, but he was sure he could time the opening.

He waited, patiently observing the legs of the guards he could see. Once the time was right, he quickly pushed himself off the ground and promptly moved over to the edge of the commander's tent. He took a quick glance around to make sure no one saw him before he pulled one of the tent spikes out, lifted the edge of the fabric, and slipped underneath to get inside.

As he popped his head inside, he was relieved to see there were no guards posted within, which was something he realized he had failed to consider. He put his shortsightedness behind him and started looking around for anything that might be useful.

All around the room, there were plenty of ornate items on shelves and desks. The tent was set up like a permanent living arrangement, even though it had only been there for the last few weeks. However, it appeared to be in the process of being packed, which gave credence to the rumor that they would be leaving soon.

Among the items strewn about was a journal on the desk. Dante grabbed the journal and started to thumb through the pages to see if there was anything useful, but it was mainly just the tired rantings of an old soldier who was stuck at a post he hated with soldiers he felt didn't listen. However, a sealed envelope on the desk caught his attention; it looked very important.

Dante set the notebook down where he found it and grabbed the envelope. He saw that the wax seal was the same insignia the knights wore, the symbol of King Damon, so he knew it was an official document. He pried open the wax seal, doing his best not to break it, but it fell apart almost immediately.

"Shit," Dante thought to himself as he grabbed the small pieces of wax and put them in his pocket, "What a clumsy ass. Now there's no pretending I didn't open it."

He cleaned up his mess quickly, leaving no trace or evidence behind him, and then went back to looking at the letter. He glanced it over for a moment, skimming for anything that would jump out at him, and his eyes widened. He rapidly folded the letter and placed it in his pocket, as he had found what he came looking for.

Dante turned to leave the same way he entered when he heard someone approaching the tent. He knew he wouldn't be able to get out without getting caught, so he scrambled to hide underneath the desk. He tucked himself away as deeply as he could and then froze himself into place as he made his breathing silent.

He could hear his heart beating in his ears as his anxiety shot through the ceiling. Every noise was deafening, and he felt hyperaware of every little detail. He knew getting caught would mean he didn't leave the tent, so he had no choice but to remain calm.

Whoever entered the tent walked over to the desk and grabbed the chair. They threw their legs in front and slid the chair into position. Dante watched in terror as he recognized the boots to be none other than the commander's. As the commander scooted into position, his boot nearly struck Dante in the head, but he stopped just short.

Dante's heart skipped a beat, and he observed the commander's legs closely, trying desperately to avoid any contact. He could hear the commander ruffling around on the desk, and then he started to ruffle around in the drawers.

"What the hells? Where did I put it?" the commander mumbled to himself.

"Damnit," Dante worried to himself in a panic, "He's talking about this letter!"

The commander continued to rummage around, growing more and more frantic as he searched through his things. Once he realized it wasn't where he left it, he started to scoot the chair back away from the desk.

"He's going to look under the desk," Dante said as his breathing began to accelerate.

The commander braced himself on the desk and started to lean down to see if the paper had fallen underneath his feet. Dante could see the decorations on his chest and began to catastrophise. He wondered how the commander would kill him, or if there was any way he could talk himself out of this situation. His head began to feel light, and he was about to pass out when he heard someone burst into the tent.

"Commander!" a voice yelled, startling both Dante and the commander.

Dante let out a sharp gasp, and his eyes flared wide open. The next second felt like it dragged on for an hour before he heard the commander speak.

"What is it?" the commander barked, returning to an upright position.

"You're needed with the quartermaster, sir. He said it's time to look over provisioning to ensure we have enough for the campaign ahead," the voice from the doorway responded.

The commander let out a long sigh and mumbled to himself as he stood to his feet, "I can't get a moment of peace around here. Bunch of lazy, incompetent bastards."

The commander and the other man exited the tent, leaving a horrified Dante in place, wondering how he was still alive. Dante waited a moment to make sure he was alone, and then quickly scurried over to the part of the tent he had entered through. He poked his head out of the other side and made sure no one was watching before he slipped back out.

He drove the tent stake back in and then casually strolled away from the camp.

Once he was in the grass, he would be clear of any arguments about coming near the camp, so he didn't stress about it and didn't need to crawl back the same way he approached. It took him significantly less time to get back onto the road in the village and away from harm's way.

"That was way too close," Dante thought as he walked through the village streets, his hands still shaking from the close brush with death. "One wrong move and I would have been a dead man. Ohoho, wait until Aslan hears about this. Now I can at least add sneaky to my abilities." A smile crept across Dante's face as he thought about it, "Y'know, maybe I'm not so useless after all. I mean, I doubt any of them landed this kind of information. I can contribute."

His chin was held high for the first time in a long time, and he was excited to feel like he was actually worth a spot in the group he had called home for most of his life. So, with anticipation brimming at the front of his mind, he patiently waited for the sun to begin descending before he started to regroup with everyone else.

Chapter 4

Throughout the rest of the day, Dante could tell the knights were on edge. The commander was upset that he had misplaced the King's letter, and his anger was passed down the ranks. Dante couldn't care less about that, as long as they didn't suspect or catch onto him.

He avoided contact with them the rest of the evening, as he didn't want to allow any opportunities for conflict. He knew he was only a few hours away from meeting with the others, and he didn't want to cause any problems with their plan.

The time ticked by painstakingly slowly. Dante did his best to pass the minutes by looking for anything that may require attention. He diligently searched the marketplace for thieves, scanned the village's perimeter for prying eyes, and even asked around the village if any chores needed finishing. Whatever it took to make the sun fall.

After a few small chores and a lot of pacing around, the sun was finally beginning to retreat behind the trees, and Dante started making his way toward Faetu's house. He weaved through the village, left turn after right turn, until he arrived at the door. He gave the entrance a slight tap as he let himself in, to let them know he had made it.

"About time you showed up," Aslan teased.

"Was I really the last one?" Dante asked. "I thought we were meeting at nightfall, the sun has barely gone down."

"You're perfectly fine," Aliyah assured. "We haven't been here long. Come, have a seat."

"Okay, now that we're all here, I want to know what you know," Faetu declared. "We'll do this one at a time, but I have some things that may help us plan."

Faetu took everything on his table and set it aside before pulling out a large map of the area. The map stretched from the village of Miradoor, all the way down to the small town of Greenfell. It was a large map, but it was needed to display the sheer size of Damon's empire.

"We can use this to plot points that we have, and maybe see a good plan unfold right before our eyes. I don't know about you guys, but I'm a visual learner," Faetu explained.

"Well, since we're getting fancy, I'll go first," Aslan stated as he pulled some documents from his bag and set them on the edge of the map. He pointed to a fortified city that was northwest of Greenfell and sat along the coast, saying, "That is Blackhold, a major city in the southern region. It is pretty far outside of King Damon's borders, but there really isn't much between them except for a couple of small villages."

"Okay? What are the documents for?" Aliyah asked.

"These are battle plans for the armies of the Devalon Empire, soldiers of King Damon. It's a detailed layout of how he plans to take over Blackhold. I slipped these out of some loose pockets earlier today. If he's trying to take over Blackhold, tens of thousands of people are about to die. This military feat alone would be incredibly difficult, let alone the task of successfully occupying the city afterward. I don't understand what he hopes to accomplish, but he has bloodshed in his plans for sure," Aslan stated.

"Do they say anything about the time he plans to be there or when he plans on leading the assault?" Dante asked.

"No, they're just the skeleton plans. I'm assuming he is preparing for an operation that he's likely to implement within the next few years," Aslan answered.

"This's good, at least we know what his end goals are," Faetu observed aloud.

"What about you? What did you find?" Aslan asked Faetu.

"I actually feel like I didn't gather much at all," Faetu answered. "I looked all day, but the only information I was able to get was where the troops are currently starting to concentrate. But that doesn't really give us much to go on. I was really hoping you guys found more than I did."

"Wasn't this whole thing your idea?" Aslan teased.

"And you barely even got any information," Aliyah continued.

"Hey, I think this could be useful," Dante disagreed. "If we know where the troops are weakest, then we could easily path our travel plans to avoid any potential conflict."

"Thank you, Dante," Faetu said with a nod. He looked at Aliyah and asked. "Besides, what information do you have?"

"I have some extra juicy information," Aliyah said with an eyebrow raised.

"Spit it out then," Aslan grumbled.

"I learned what King Damon is *really* after," Aliyah continued. "He's after a great and powerful dragon."

"What does he want with a dragon?" Dante asked.

"Apparently, a dragon named Kavronax completely wiped out a standing army of Damon's. Around a thousand knights were killed in minutes as the dragon tore through them, consuming them for energy and flying off to the south," Aliyah answered.

"Kavronax the Vile…" Aslan muttered. "I've heard of that dragon before. He's been around for lifetimes and killed more people than any of us could count. He has a reputation for destroying cities for no reason other than to watch them burn."

"Personal experience?" Faetu asked.

"Nah, thankfully. But I have heard plenty of people talking about it while I was traveling. He has become a legend in the area, and a bad omen to see in the clouds," Aslan stated.

"Well, King Damon wants to kill him, apparently, he views Kavronax's existence as a slight against his might and wants to dispose of the legendary creature," Aliyah explained.

"We should just let him go after Kavronax, then the dragon will take care of him for us," Aslan said with a laugh.

"If that were a guarantee, I would agree, but if Damon pulled it off, he could potentially grow incredibly in strength. If that were to happen, we would struggle to accomplish our goal," Faetu warned.

"Yeah, you're probably right," Aslan agreed.

"Knowing our luck, he would have some sort of dragon-harvesting weapon that would consume Kavronax and turn Damon into a god," Dante said sarcastically.

"That would definitely be unfortunate," Aliyah said with a laugh.

"Okay, what can we do with this information?" Faetu asked, looking down at what was on the table.

Kinomaru gently leaned forward and placed a small gold coin on the map. The coin was part of King Damon's currency and had his symbol facing up on the map.

"What is this?" Faetu asked.

"You know, if you just talked, this whole process would be so much smoother," Aslan sighed.

"Are you saying something is there?" Faetu asked as he looked specifically at the location Kinomaru placed the coin.

"Wait, isn't that where Damon's prison mine is?" Dante asked as he slid the coin to the side to look at the map.

"Yeah, you're right," Aslan agreed.

Aliyah looked closely at the coin, then at the map, and then realized what Kinomaru was trying to tell them. She blurted, "Are you telling us King Damon is there?"

Kinomaru smiled gently and leaned back into his seat, confirming what she said. He then grabbed his bowl of food and continued eating as the others discussed what he had found.

"This is great news," Faetu exclaimed. "I don't know how the hells you figured that out, but thank you, Kinomaru. Now all we need is to find the right place to snag him."

"It's funny you mention that," Dante said as he reached into his pocket and pulled out the letter he stole from the commander. "Have a look at this."

Faetu took the letter and read it over, his eyes widened as the information jumped from the page. A smile stretched across his face before he slowly set the letter down and looked at Dante in pleasant disbelief.

"Where did you find this?" Faetu asked.

"I slipped into the commander's tent and snagged it," Dante answered.

"You madman," Faetu said with a hearty laugh. "What were you thinking? They would have killed you if they found you."

"I was almost caught, too," Dante laughed nervously.

"You are crazy," Aliyah chuckled.

"Well, enlighten the rest of us, what does the letter say?" Aslan asked.

"It is an official order for the commanders to meet with King Damon. It has the location, date, and time. This gives us the exact time King Damon will leave the prison and start for the meeting point. Now all we have to do is find a point along this road, and we'll be able to pick our ambush spot," Faetu trailed off as he started to follow the road from the prison.

Everyone looked intently at the map as Faetu ran his finger along the path King Damon would be traveling. He eventually settled on a spot along the map and said, "There. That is where we will put an end to all of this."

"What's there?" Dante asked.

"I have traveled to Angelwood before, and this point in the road is exceptionally difficult to see ahead of you. It's covered in a dense canopy that arches over the roadway and conceals anything that may be good at hiding in the trees. It's a perfect place for us to set our trap," Faetu explained.

"When do we leave?" Aslan asked.

"Well, we were planning on having some fun this weekend, so why don't we leave now and get there before then?" Faetu suggested.

"What about Hendrickson? What are we going to tell him?" Dante asked.

"I've already spoken with him," Faetu answered.

"What? What did he say?" Aliyah asked.

"I told him that we are all leaving, and that it was better if he didn't know why. I don't know if he understood what I meant, or if he truly didn't care, but he stopped asking any questions. He told us to be safe and to stay out of trouble, that he would cover our guard shifts until the rotation could be sorted out," Faetu answered.

"You think he knows what we're planning?" Aliyah asked.

"I'm certain of it," Dante stated. "He is surprisingly perceptive for an old man. I'm surprised he didn't try to talk you out of it."

"Either way, we're cleared to leave, and we don't have to sneak out to do it," Faetu stated. "We can come back and ask for forgiveness after we're done. At least we'll be out from under the blanket of violence Damon has laid over us."

"I'm ready whenever you are. Let's take down a monarch," Aslan said with confidence.

"I've already packed up plenty of rations. We can leave now if we want to," Aliyah stated.

"I say let's do it," Dante agreed.

"You ready, big guy?" Faetu asked as he looked at Kinomaru.

Their silent friend nodded slightly and slowly stood from his chair. Everyone else did the same and started gathering their things for the journey.

"That settles it then, today marks day one of our monumental journey. We're going to free these lands and become heroes," Faetu said with pride.

The five young adventurers left Faetu's home with purpose in their hearts. They gathered up everything they would need: food, supplies, and equipment, and then returned to Faetu's house to get a little rest before leaving.

They only slept for a short time before waking back up and leaving Dawnberry. They wanted to start their journey before daybreak to avoid suspicion, questions, or interruptions. They had a long trip ahead of them, and the sooner they started, the better.

By the time the sun's rays started to peek over the tops of the eastern mountains, the group was already miles from Dawnberry. They estimated it would take them about five days to reach their ambush point, so they prepared for the long haul.

As the sun began to warm their skin, they gained a clearer view of their surroundings and felt free of any shackles or chains. Walking through nature felt like they had escaped any worries, and they were genuinely enjoying themselves. They laughed and even playfully chased one another from time to time. The trip was starting pleasantly and heartwarming, and they were happy about it.

They would walk during the day, soaking in their surroundings, observing the wildlife, and covering as much ground as possible. At night, they set up camp and nestled into their sleeping arrangements for a good night's rest. They were all lying around the campfire when Faetu broke the peaceful silence.

"Hey, what are you guys going to do after we're free from all this?" Faetu asked.

"What do you mean?" Aliyah asked.

"I mean, what will you do once Damon is no longer around?" Faetu clarified.

"Well, I haven't really thought about it," Aliyah answered.

"I guess I planned just to go back to Dawnberry. Go back to what we were doing before, except this time we don't have to deal with the knights all the time," Dante answered.

"You have to dream big," Aslan said as he looked up at the stars. "Why go back to Dawnberry? We could strike out and make a name for ourselves as vanquishers of evil."

"You mean mercenaries?" Aliyah asked.

"Well, yeah. We have to make gold somehow. Even warriors of virtue need to eat," Aslan defended.

"I don't know. Adventuring sounds exciting, but I think it would be nice to settle down peacefully," Dante disagreed.

"I think I am in the same boat as you. It would be nice to go back to Dawnberry without the fear of the knights or King Damon. Even if we didn't go there, maybe we could find a different town or a new place to explore while still making a home. Yeah, that would be nice," Aliyah said as she seemed lost in thought.

Hearing her words warmed Dante's heart. Despite his hesitance to ever voice how he feels, it made him happy to know that their future goals were at least similar.

"Well, I think I know what I'm going to do," Faetu spoke.

"What is that?" Aslan asked.

"I'm going to be King," Faetu answered confidently.

"What?" Dante asked in confusion.

"That's a bold aspiration," Aslan said with a chuckle. "What makes you think you're King material?"

"I think he's King material," Aliyah said in admiration.

"I don't think the people need King material, I think they need a leader that cares, one that can lead by example instead of violence. I think I can fill that role, and I want to show everyone that a King doesn't have to be a tyrant," Faetu proclaimed.

"Well, I wish you luck with that," Dante dismissed. "Too much political nonsense for me. I'm willing to bet that being King isn't as simple as it sounds."

"I'm certain it isn't, but I'm also certain I want to try," Faetu said with a smile.

"After we're done here, there will be an open seat, so feel free to take it," Aslan said as he rolled over to get comfortable. "As for me, I'm going to sleep."

"I second that," Dante added. "You alright over there, Kinomaru?"

Kinomaru looked at him with a grin from his sleeping mat and nestled himself deeper into position to get more comfortable.

Dante nodded and said, "I'm glad. Good night, everyone."

Everybody else said their goodnights and nuzzled into sleep. The cool air around them made drifting off into slumber much easier than they'd thought, but the ground still wasn't the most comfortable. Despite this, they all got a good night's rest and woke the next morning feeling refreshed and ready to continue their journey.

The first days were similarly pleasant, filled with beautiful landscapes and welcoming environments, but that changed once they reached farther south. The once-green landscapes began to look gray and lifeless. A thin layer of smoke slowly began to nestle along the ground for miles in every direction. This was alarming at first, but the alarm quickly turned to horror as they continued south.

As they pressed onward, the smell of smoke grew thicker, carrying a faint copper tinge with it. The smell was immediately familiar to them; it was the smell of blood, and they stumbled into the source quickly. Deep within the blanket of smoke, a scene of horrors unfolded. Bodies littered the field and blood stained the grass beneath their feet. It was a massacre.

Hundreds of corpses, dressed in regular clothing, were scattered all around them. There were men, women, children, and even animals among the deceased. All of them appeared to have met their death at the end of a blade.

"What happened here?" Aliyah asked in shock.

"This would be Damon's doing," Faetu answered through clenched teeth.

"These poor bastards," Aslan muttered, "They never stood a chance."

"They're not even soldiers," Dante observed aloud.

"No, they're likely villagers who refused to bend to Damon's will," Faetu responded. "He slaughters anyone who doesn't fall in line."

"How could someone do something like this?" Aliyah asked.

"Only someone devoid of morals or human nature is capable of this. Only a monster," Faetu answered. "This would have been us if Hendrickson hadn't groveled at his feet."

"He will pay for this," Dante grumbled as he stepped over the body of a peasant woman.

"With his life," Faetu agreed.

"Should we do something for these people?" Aliyah asked.

"The only thing we can do for them is get vengeance," Aslan stated. "There are too many to lay to rest; we'd be here for weeks."

"He's right," Dante added. "Besides, if we stall, we will miss our window to ambush Damon."

"We will press onward. And once we end Damon's reign, we can come back to pay respects to the lives lost here," Faetu stated.

They continued to march through the sea of the dead, trying their best not to look into the eyes of the bodies. Each time they unintentionally glanced down, the eyes of the dead felt like they were watching. It felt like they stared up at them with despair, begging for help. They kept their heads forward and did their best to stay focused. However, the scene really rattled them. Despite their ambitions to kill the King, they were not veterans of battle. None of them had seen an actual battle between armies in their lives, and the goal of their quest was beginning to feel out of reach.

"Hundreds of people, killed mercilessly," Dante thought to himself, "Just like in Dawnberry. How many times has this bastard done this? How many people has he killed? How many more will he kill if we don't stop him? How many orphans has he created?"

"Dante, are you okay?" Aliyah asked as she nudged his shoulder.

Dante's attention snapped to her as he shook his head. He quickly looked around and noticed he was falling behind, and he said, "Um, yeah, I'm fine. I'm sorry."

"You seem flustered. Are you sure you're okay?" Aliyah asked again.

"Yes, I promise," Dante said with a light sigh as Aliyah's words felt like a warm blanket that wrapped around his body. "I was just lost in thought is all."

"Okay, well, if you need anything, don't hesitate to speak up," Aliyah offered.

"Thank you," Dante said with a grin and a nod. He thought to himself, "Her words are like an antidote to my worries. How is someone so beautiful also so incredibly warm to be around?"

"Let's keep going, we're almost to the ambush spot. It should only be another half day's travel from here, though we will likely have to stop before we get there to make camp," Faetu instructed.

Everyone agreed and picked up the pace. They wanted to arrive quickly, but also wanted to put distance between themselves and the field of nightmares they stumbled into. It took little time for them to reach the other side of the massacre. However, they didn't carry the same mentality the remainder of the journey.

The once-happy feeling that rested in their chests as they walked was replaced by anger and worry. They felt free at the beginning, but that feeling was replaced with a sense of duty, an obligation to bring down the great evil atop the mountain of death and fear. The scab that had grown over the old wounds created by King Damon all those years ago was ripped off, and the emotions flowed free once again.

These feelings stirred within them and gave them motivation to push onward. They gave them fuel to want the King dead for everything he had done. But more than anything else, they began to wonder if they were going to die before the sun set the next day.

Chapter 5

They approached a bend in the middle of the road around lunchtime the following day. They had primarily stayed silent as they walked, the weight of the scene of horrors they had witnessed the day before still sat heavily on their shoulders. The air felt clean and refreshing, but the tension was thick enough to cut.

"This is the place," Faetu stated. "This is where we will kill Damon."

"We could hide right there," Aslan said as he pointed to some bushes just off the road. "The wagon won't be able to see us as it approaches, but we'll be able to see it coming from pretty far away."

"Then let's settle in and get comfortable. We may be here a day or two, depending on how long it takes Damon to come through here, but we will see him eventually."

They all walked over to the hiding spot and settled in for a long wait. Their nerves were high, and they knew a fight was ahead of them, but they had come too far to back away now. They all watched the road intently for an hour before their nerves began to calm down a bit. Everyone except Aslan began to relax, but he seemed to grow more anxious as time went on.

"I have a bad feeling about this, guys," Aslan stated suddenly, breaking the silence.

"Why so?" Aliyah asked.

"I don't know, but it feels like every cell in my body is telling me to leave. I think we should go and come back when we have a different plan, maybe recruit more help," Aslan suggested.

"I can't say I disagree. More help could be a good thing," Dante agreed.

"No, I'm not leaving," Faetu dismissed.

"I understand you want to take down Damon, more than anyone else," Dante said. "But maybe it would be better to enlist some help from a nearby village?"

"No, it's too late," Faetu argued.

"Why is it too late?" Aslan stated.

"Because there he is," Faetu said as he looked through his brow toward the end of the road.

Coming around the corner, a fair distance down the road, was a wagon that was far from ordinary. The wagon, pulled by four white horses, was draped in fine armor and pristine fabric. The carriage itself was ornately crafted but covered in plate armor, clearly designed to repel incoming attacks.

"Keep your heads down and stay quiet," Faetu whispered. "If you want to run, wait until the fighting starts."

Everyone nervously waited as the wagon slowly trotted closer and closer. There were no guards outside of the wagon, and whoever had the reins was sitting behind an iron-plated cover with nothing more than a thin slit to see out of. They couldn't see if King Damon was inside.

The seconds felt like hours as the wagon drew closer with each passing moment. Everyone prepared themselves for the fight of their lives as they took a firm grip on their weapons and waited patiently for their opportunity to strike.

"Listen," Faetu whispered. "When the wagon draws near, focus on the horses. If we kill them, they can't escape, and we'll have our target. There's no way we can get through that armor before they flee. Even better if you can hit the driver through that slit, Aliyah."

"I'm a pretty good shot, but that would take a great deal of luck as well," Aliyah whispered back. "Let's not rely on it."

"Once we stop the wagon, Kinomaru can take his hammer and beat his way inside," Faetu instructed. "Aslan, Dante, and I will kill the horses."

"Understood," Dante said as he let out a slow breath to calm himself and situated his grip. He looked at the wagon and thought, "This is finally it. There's no running back now. All we have to do is kill one man, and the worries of the people are over. There are five of us; how hard can that be? It's comforting to know I'm not the only one nervous about all this, but something's not right with Faetu. Maybe it's because I've known him for so long, but something isn't right. He seems different after what we saw yesterday, he seems… afraid."

"Get ready," Faetu whispered one last time.

The wagon was nearly to the bend in the road as everyone's hearts beat out of their chests. The butterflies in their stomachs were swirling rampantly, making them almost nauseous. The anticipation was murderous as they watched the wagon slow to a stop just before it reached the ambush point.

"Wait, what?" Dante thought to himself. "Why did it stop?"

Before he could say anything, the feeling of cold steel pressed against his throat. He froze in place, thinking for sure he was dead, but the blade rested against his skin, unmoving. He looked down to see a shortsword at his throat, and then noticed that everyone else was in the same situation. Five people, all identical to one another, seemed to appear out of nowhere and had each of them trapped. They were all wearing hooded cloaks and held a walking staff in one hand. They were shadowy and their identities veiled, yet they appeared impossible to tell apart. One move and they were dead.

"Shit," Aslan muttered in a shaky voice. "I knew we should have left."

"Shut up," one of the men demanded. "On your feet, keep your weapons."

All five of them slowly stood to their feet with the blades remaining pressed against their throats as a countermeasure to any plans they may have had. They were escorted out of the bushes and into the road in front of the wagon. The men kicked each of them behind the knees to force them to the ground and lined all five of them up in a row.

"Lay your weapons in front of you," the shadowy men ordered. "Then place your hands on your legs. If they move, you will be killed."

The group did as they were told and set their weapons down on the ground. They were terrified of whatever was coming next, and they all wore that expression except Faetu. He appeared unbothered by everything happening and stared at the wagon with hate in his eyes.

Suddenly, the wagon door swung open. The creaky hinges sliced through the silence, sounding much louder than they actually were. After a moment, a boot stepped out of the wagon and onto the first step, followed by another. King Damon stood up on the first step and stretched his arms out as if he had been sleeping. Then he looked over at the group on the ground in front of him with a smile on his face.

Each step he took sounded louder than the last as he walked down the carriage steps and onto the road. Then he slowly walked over to the group, looking carefully at each of them.

"Normally, people hiding in bushes are killed on sight. I typically don't bother myself with distinguishing between assassins and cowards, as neither of them is useful to me. However, I just had a meeting with an old friend, so I'm in a good mood. This is good news for each of you," Damon said as he stood in front of each of them. "I can tell you're the muscle," Damon said as he pointed to Kinomaru. He pointed at Aliyah and said, "and you're the healer. You're the rogue," he said as he pointed to Aslan. He paused for a moment as he looked at Dante, who was beside Faetu, and said, "You are who I'm perplexed about. It's obvious that the next guy is the leader of this embarrassing group of would-be assassins, but what are you here for? It would seem your leader is everything you are but better, so I wonder why they brought you along. Maybe out of pity."

Damon paused for a bit longer as he continued to observe each of the people before him. Finally, he broke the silence once again as he knelt in front of Faetu and said, "So, fearless leader, why are you here?"

"We've come to kill you," Faetu answered as he stared King Damon in the eyes.

"Oh, I know that much already. I can see it in your eyes, you want to grab this sword and strike me down," Damon taunted. He grabbed Faetu's sword and pushed it closer to him, saying, "Go ahead, try it."

Faetu didn't move. He wanted to grab the sword, but he knew it was a trap. The moment he reached for it, the people behind him would cut him down, so he simply sat still and waited.

"You know what else I can see in your eyes?" Damon asked rhetorically, "Fear."

"I'm not afraid of you," Faetu stated defensively.

"Oh no, dear boy, I know you aren't afraid of me, but you're afraid of what I deal. You are afraid of death. You can lie to yourself, you can lie to your friends, but you can't lie to me. You're terrified you're not going to live to see another day," Damon explained coldly. "In fact, all of you are, except your big friend at the end."

Damon stood back up and began to pace back and forth in front of the group as he spoke, "You know, elves make a great scouting party, especially this guy. Their footsteps are silent, so they can move exceptionally quietly; fools like you don't see them coming. Can you believe all of these men are the same person? Who you're looking at is the most deadly blade in history. He has killed so many people that even I couldn't begin to compare. You don't earn a name like the Merchant of Death for nothing. I... borrowed him from the Hallowed Shroud. Have you heard of the Hallowed Shroud? Never mind, don't answer that, I know you haven't. If the most deadly assassin in the world works for me, what drove the likes of you even to attempt this?"

Damon paused again, this time his expression shifted from carefree to almost gleeful. A smirk stretched across his face until it grew to a devilish grin. He seemed to be lost in a great idea for a moment before he finally broke the silence once again.

"You know, I'm feeling incredibly generous today. All of you, pick up your weapons," Damon ordered.

The group looked confused and hesitated, not wanting to fall for his trap. They didn't remove their hands from their legs and kept their eyes trained on the ground in front of them.

"I don't believe you heard me clearly. I will not tell you again, pick up your weapons and stand. If you ignore me, I will have all of you killed before a single one of your filthy corpses hits the ground," Damon snarled.

Their hearts started to beat out of their chests as they feared what was to come next. Faetu was the first to reach for his sword, followed by everyone else. Dante was the last; he was starting to panic internally as worry took control of his body. His hands trembled as he reached for his sword, and his palms were covered in sweat as he tried to get a better grip on his weapon.

"We're going to die here," Dante thought. "We came all this way just to die. I'll never get to see Dawnberry at peace, I'll never get to tell Aliyah how I feel, and I'll never get to grow old and start a family. I can barely hold my sword. How am I supposed to fight like this?"

"Snap out of it, Dante," Faetu said as he stood with his weapon in hand. "No matter what happens, I know you have greatness within you. But you need to breathe and calm your nerves; you'll never be able to win if you panic."

"Right," Dante agreed as he tried to take a steady breath and stand up. He was still far from calm, but Faetu's words helped him relax enough to get a hold of himself.

"Now, you've come here to kill me, so do it," Damon ordered.

He waited for a few seconds, but no one budged; they just stood in place with their weapons at the ready. Damon started to laugh at the sight, finding their fear incredibly amusing.

"You should be embarrassed. Not only do you look inexperienced and underprepared, but you also get the chance to do what you came to do, and you stand frozen like a statue. This is the opportunity you wanted, isn't it? You five against the King, good against evil, a battle of fates, yet you don't act. If you're worried about my friend stepping in, he won't. In fact, if you manage to kill me, he will let you go free. So, hit me with your best shot, I could use a warmup," Damon taunted.

Everyone stood ready to attack, but they weren't sure how to approach King Damon. His true abilities were unknown to them, so they didn't want to leave themselves open. Faetu strategized as much as he could, desperately searching for a way to take Damon down, but was struggling to come up with a safe approach. As he stared, he saw that Aslan had started to move out of the corner of his eye.

"Enough waiting around," Aslan shouted as he ran toward Damon with a sword in each hand. "Let's get this over with. We will either die or kill this bastard and go home."

Faetu surged his power into his weapon and coated the blade with flames that burned hot enough to cut through iron. Aliyah grabbed her bow and drew an arrow, Kinomaru started to approach with his hammer in his hand, and Dante readied his longsword with trembling fingers.

Everyone was ready to charge at Damon, but Aslan got to him first. Aslan jumped and swung his blade toward Damon's neck, but the King didn't seem to flinch. Instead, Aslan felt a sharp pain and then warmth on his chest. He landed and saw his blade tumble across the ground, severed from the hilt of his weapon. He quickly turned around to see that Damon didn't have a scratch on him.

"ASLAN!" Faetu shouted.

Aslan dropped his broken weapon and readied his second one, determined to land a blow, but then he started to panic. He felt like he hadn't taken a breath, but he wasn't able to when he tried. He looked down to see that his coat was covered in blood, and then he grabbed his neck to find it had been sliced open. His eyes grew wide as he felt blood pouring over his fingertips.

"What's the matter? Not as easy as you expected it to be?" Damon taunted as he relished in Aslan's panic.

Aslan could feel his body getting weak. His vision was rapidly becoming hazy, and he knew he had lost a lot of blood already. He quickly started to run back toward Aliyah, hoping she could heal the wound, while the rest of the group began to attack.

Faetu approached quickly but carefully, trying to avoid being cut like Aslan had been. He swung his blade toward Damon's head, but the King easily deflected the attack and knocked Faetu off balance. Damon leaned back to avoid a massive swing from Kinomaru's hammer before kicking Dante's hands to knock his sword out of his grasp.

While everyone was off balance, Damon attacked. He slammed a knee upward into Faetu's ribs, backhanded Dante to knock him to the ground, stabbed his blade into Kinomaru's thigh, then slammed a thunderous punch downward into Faetu's head.

"I got you, Aslan," Aliyah said in a panic as she immediately started trying to heal her friend's wounds.

She placed her hand on his neck and started trying to seal the wound and mend the tissue. The bleeding was the first thing she stopped, but she was having trouble getting the gash on his neck to close. Despite her abilities, she was not the best healer in the world, and it took her time to mend severe injuries.

Damon saw that Aslan had reached Aliyah and realized the extent of her healing powers. He held his hand out in front of him and muttered, "No, you don't."

A powerful stream of grey-tinted magic ripped across the ground as it blasted from his hand at incredible speed. The projectile was like a rail cannon as it kicked up dust around him as it rocketed toward them. The attack was thunderously loud, incredibly precise, and inhumanly fast.

Aslan saw Damon's attack and reacted as fast as he could. He shoved Aliyah away and tried to lean back to avoid the attack, but he wasn't fast enough. Aliyah watched as the attack blasted into the side of Aslan's head, ripping his face off as it removed the front third of his skull, splattering her with his blood. Aslan's body immediately crumpled to the ground as what was left of his blood began to pool under his body.

Aliyah stared at him in shock. She couldn't believe what she just saw, and tears welled up in her eyes immediately. In an instant, years of companionship were gone, and there wouldn't be another day for them to make any more memories. Aslan was dead, and there was nothing she could do about it.

"Hmph," Damon huffed as he saw the healer get saved.

"Damn you, DAMON!" Faetu shouted as he jumped up and swung his blade toward the King's chin.

Damon easily avoided the attack, but the flames on Faetu's sword were burning so hot that the metal the blade was forged out of began to deteriorate. A small droplet of molten steel flew from the blade and landed on Damon's cheek, burning his flesh.

Damon winced in pain before he had to jump backward to avoid a downward strike from Kinomaru. The weighted hammer slammed into the ground where he was standing and fractured the soil in a way that shouldn't be possible. Chunks of earth kicked up around the hammer, putting Kinomaru's strength on full display. The silent giant quickly recovered his stance and prepared to strike again.

Dante scrambled over to his sword and grabbed the blade before he stood. His heart was racing, and he could barely make sense of what was happening. His breathing was starting to accelerate, and his heartbeat was pounding in his ears. He saw Damon jump backward from Kinomaru's swing and lunged in to attack. The tip of his blade was just about to strike the King's side when he felt like he hit solid air just inches before his target.

Damon saw Dante out of the corner of his eye and could sense his confusion by the expression on his face. Damon was amused by this, but wasted no time in slamming his blade downward toward Dante's back. Just as he was about to land the attack, he was forced to roll forward to avoid getting slammed by Kinomaru's hammer.

Damon sprang back to his feet, leaned to avoid an arrow, and brushed some dirt off his shoulder before saying, "Looks like I need to deal with you first."

Damon rushed toward Kinomaru with his palm facing forward and his hand by his side. Faetu tried to step between them and thrust his blade into Damon's chest, but the King deftly maneuvered around the blade as he spun to the side and rolled up Faetu's arm. Faetu could see the smirk on the King's face as he slipped past him and slammed his palm into Kinomaru's chin.

The attack was devastating, sending a shockwave in every direction from the point of impact. Kinomaru was lifted into the air from the force of the attack before collapsing face down in the dirt. His hammer tumbled to the side, and he wasn't moving an inch.

"Two down, three to go," Damon laughed as he ducked underneath a swing from Faetu's sword.

Aliyah sprinted toward Kinomaru as fast as she could. She was in shock from what happened to Aslan, and the blood covering her face and body kept the image as fresh in her mind as possible. She was terrified that Kinomaru would be in the same state, so she kept running as fast as her legs would carry her.

Damon parried an attack from Dante, knocking him off balance, then deflected Faetu's attack with his bracer, but the heat from the blade instantly started to melt the armor the King was wearing. Damon grunted in pain as he flung the blade to the side and swayed to avoid the molten steel that fell from the weapon. Then he saw Aliyah running toward Kinomaru and reacted quickly.

Damon didn't have the time or space to launch another attack like the one he hit Aslan with, but he did throw his hand forward and sent three streaming projectiles of forceful magic twisting through the air as they spun around one another violently. The attack slammed into Aliyah, hitting her in the leg, chest, and face. Aliyah crumpled to the ground and ragdolled until she slid to a stop just a few feet away from Kinomaru.

Dante saw Aliyah hit the ground and was overcome with an anger he hadn't felt before in his entire life. He yelled loudly as he twisted around and tried to swipe his blade across Damon's face, but again the attack felt like it struck solid air just inches before him. Dante continued to scream as he poured everything he had into the swing, and suddenly the blade started to jerk closer to Damon.

The King saw the blade edging nearer to his face, and a look of slight confusion crept into his eyes as he looked at the blade and then the young man wielding it. He quickly leaned back and let the sword pass by him before he delivered a thunderous uppercut to Dante's abdomen. He followed the uppercut with another to his chin, grabbed him by his hair, slammed the pommel of his sword into his nose, kneed him in the stomach, kneed him in the face, and then let go of his hair to kick him in the chest.

Dante felt like a giant had stepped on him. His body was in pain, and he could barely move without agonizing shockwaves pulsing throughout his entire body. He struggled to push himself back to his knees, but his body was failing him. All he could do was watch Faetu as he tried his best to gather his strength.

"What the hell is he hitting me with?" Dante wondered. "It's like his punches are followed by some sort of shockwave. It's tearing at my insides with each strike. And then there's some sort of force field around him that I can't seem to get through. Just what is this guy capable of? Damnit, I have to get up. I have to grab my sword and keep fighting."

Faetu swiped his blade downward at Damon's head, but the King jumped sideways to avoid it. Molten steel was being flung with every swing, so Damon was forced to avoid the strikes as best as he could. The King ducked underneath a horizontal swing and lunged in to deliver a thunderous punch to Faetu's abdomen, knocking the wind out of him.

Faetu felt his body reeling in pain, and struggled to take in a breath as it felt like his diaphragm shut down entirely. However, he saw his opening to strike. He quickly rotated his blade and slammed it downward toward Damon's back until he felt the hand guard slam against his back. Through shallow and labored breathing, Faetu smiled at his success.

However, Faetu quickly noticed something wasn't right. He jerked his sword away from the King to reveal that his blade was gone. The heat from his flames had melted the steel completely, leaving him with nothing but the handle. He no longer had a weapon.

Damon reached down and grabbed Faetu's ankle, jerking his leg sideways and rotating him into the air. While Faetu was suspended in front of him, Damon delivered a rib-crunching punch that echoed off the trees and sent Faetu flying away until he tumbled to a stop.

Faetu slowly crawled back to his feet as he saw blood falling to the ground underneath him. He wasn't sure where it was coming from, but it didn't matter. To him, this was his last chance to kill the King. He was sure he wouldn't get back up if he took another series of blows like he just did. He saw Aliyah crumpled next to Kinomaru, he saw Dante struggling to get back up, and he saw Aslan's body lying in a bloody heap.

"Damn you, Damon," Faetu growled as he slowly made his way upright. "You will die a thousand deaths for what you've done. All the lives you've ruined and the years you've stolen will come back on you tenfold."

"Many before you have tried, and they all suffered the same fate. Come, die fighting or kill yourself now, the end result will be the same," Damon said coldly.

"Fae.. tu… just… run," Dante mumbled as his hand slipped and he fell to the ground on his face.

"No," Faetu stated with conviction as he looked down at his own hands. "I told you I always have your back."

In a sudden burst of energy, Faetu lit his hand ablaze and fires burned brightly as flares spurted from his fingertips. He winced in agony as the flames immediately started to burn his flesh, but he did his best to ignore the pain. He ran toward Damon as fast as he could and threw a quick jab as he closed the distance.

Damon leaned to the side to avoid it and repaid the attack with a powerful punch to Faetu's ribs, breaking four of them in the process. Faetu winced but quickly swung a lightning-fast overhand that managed to catch Damon on the end of his chin. Damon grew angry at the attack and went on the offensive. He swayed to avoid a follow-up punch and kicked Faetu thunderously in the abdomen, forcing him to keel over from the pain. As Faetu leaned forward, Damon slammed the pommel of his sword into the back of Faetu's head before kicking him in the side of the face and knocking him to the ground.

Faetu crumpled to the dirt. His hands no longer hurt, but that was due to the nerve damage to his flesh. He couldn't even feel them anymore. He tried his best to get to his feet, but Damon kicked him in the side every time he pushed himself up.

"You're persistent, I'll give you that, but you're persistence doesn't make you any less of a fool. You'll never be strong enough to defeat me, and you'll never get the chance to try again. Each day you've lived is nothing more than wasted air for those of us actually worth something. You came into this world worthless, helpless, covered in blood, and you are going to leave it the same way," Damon threatened.

Faetu managed to push himself up to his knees, sitting on his feet. His hands were mangled, and blood fell from multiple places along his body. Each breath was agonizing, as he was sure almost all of his ribs were broken. He looked over to see that Dante was staring at him with terror in his eyes.

"Close your eyes," Faetu mumbled as he looked at Dante and smiled.

In the blink of an eye, Damon passed his blade completely through Faetu's neck, severing his head and ending his life in a flash. Dante just stared at him in disbelief. He couldn't bear what he was seeing. He couldn't accept what was happening to them, and he began to panic.

Dante stared at the headless body of his best friend, someone he had spent his entire life with, someone who had always been around to help him when he needed it. His breathing was shallow, and his heart pumped at an alarming rate. His stomach turned in knots as he felt like he was going to vomit. His vision began to get blurry, and his skin felt like it was on fire.

"When you see one friend die, it breaks your morale," Damon said as he slowly walked over to Dante. "When you see two friends die, it breaks your composure. When you see three friends die, it breaks your spirit. But when everyone around you is dead and you realize that no matter how hard you try, you'll never succeed. That breaks your hope. Once your hope is broken, you will never rise again."

Dante was in a daze; he could barely hear what King Damon was saying, as the sound of his own heartbeat pounded thunderously in his ear. It felt like something was clawing inside of him, but he was frozen in place. It seemed like he was going to pass out at any moment.

Damon raised his sword as he looked at Dante and was about to slice the blade into his throat when the caw of a crow rang out from the trees. Damon jumped at the sound, then looked around to see where it came from. He only looked for a brief moment before he took a step away from Dante and sheathed his sword.

Dante was beginning to feel woozy as he looked through his eyebrows at Damon. It felt like rage was coursing through his veins as the man who had taken so much from him stood comfortable and unharmed. His body felt light, and he was starting to feel a surge of energy rush through his limbs. He looked down at his sword and began to reach for it when his vision went entirely black.

Dust kicked outward in every direction as Dante crumpled to the soil. Damon shook the blood from his knuckles and then looked around at the people he had just decisively beaten. He then took an extra second to look at Dante as he thought about how such a pitiful boy was able to force his blade through his barrier.

"Check them, and take the survivors to Angron Prison," Damon ordered. "Use the trailing wagon to haul them back. We'll either get some use out of them or they'll die."

"As you wish," one of the copies answered in a sinister tone.

"What a waste of potential," Damon grumbled as he looked down at Faetu's corpse.

King Damon brushed any remaining dirt from his clothes and wiped any blood off his armor and weapons before walking back to his wagon. He took his seat where he previously was and continued his trip as if nothing had happened. He either battered or killed five people by himself and was completely unbothered by it. He acted as if it were just another day for him. Within minutes, his wagon was gone, disappearing into the distance around a bend and behind the trees.

A second wagon started pulling up and stopped to load Dante into the back. They grabbed his body and threw it into the back of the wagon, leaving him unconscious on the hardwood floor. There were only two guards on the wagon: one was outside, controlling the horses, and the other sat in the back to stand watch as they traveled.

The day was bloody and disastrous. Despite their best efforts, they were barely able to lay a finger on the King, and some of them paid with their lives. It was a brutal defeat, and they were plagued by the nightmare of living with their failure. Dante was especially distraught, as the look on Faetu's face before he died would be burned into his memory forever.

Chapter 6

Dante's eyes slowly opened to see that he was lying on a bed of grass. He looked around, and everyone was sitting next to him as they watched the morning sun rise in the distance. There was no blood, no death, and no King, just the five of them and some warm sunlight to bathe in.

Dante sat up immediately and started to panic. His eyes shot around as he tried to make sense of everything he was seeing. Faetu looked over and saw he was acting strange.

"Is everything okay, Dante?" Faetu asked.

"How are you here? I saw you die?" Dante blurted.

"What?" Aslan blurted. "You must have been having a bad dream."

"You did look like you were tossing and turning a lot just now," Aliyah added.

"As you can see, I'm clearly not dead," Faetu dismissed with a laugh. "Come on, it's time to go."

"Where are we going?" Dante asked.

"We're almost to the ambush point. We should be there by midday," Faetu answered.

"Wait, we haven't reached Damon yet?" Dante asked.

"No," Faetu answered.

"That dream really has you messed up," Aslan said with a laugh.

"You don't understand, that was more than a dream, that seemed so real," Dante argued. "I think we should turn around."

"Turn around? Why would we do that?" Faetu asked.

"We've come so far already. Why would we turn back now?" Aliyah asked as well.

"Guys, please, listen to me. If we face King Damon as we are, we will die. I just know it, I can feel it in my gut. Please, we're not strong enough yet," Dante pleaded. "I saw it happen. He killed you right in front of me."

"Dante, just breathe, I'm right here. You just had a bad dream, that's all. Damon is nothing more than a man, and a man bleeds like any other," Faetu dismissed before he chuckled. "I'm surprised your dream version of us is so weak."

Dante began to panic as he remembered everything he dreamed about, but it felt like more than a dream, almost like a premonition. He couldn't make sense of it, but it was unlike anything he had experienced before.

"Please, let's go back. We can get some more help before we attack and make sure we'll win. I don't want to watch any of you die, please, listen to me," Dante begged.

The ground beneath them began to shake abruptly, and then it stopped just as quickly as it started.

"What was that?" Dante asked.

"Quakes," Aslan answered.

"They've been happening on and off for hours. They're always short, but they've been fairly consistent," Aliyah added.

"Please, Fae-" Dante started talking before he was interrupted.

"Dante, just breathe," Faetu spoke calmly. "It doesn't matter what you say, I'm not turning back. This is what I am meant to do, I can feel it in my soul. I will confront Damon, strike him down, and become King."

"I…" Dante tried to come up with the words to say, but he couldn't. A bad dream wasn't nearly enough reason to abandon the entire mission, but he couldn't shake the feeling that something was wrong. "But Faetu, if we're wrong, we may die."

The ground shook beneath him again, this time slightly more violently than the last. Dante looked at the ground, worried, but was confused as to why no one else was. It just felt like the earth beneath them jumped upward, and no one batted an eye.

"Something's not right here," Dante thought to himself.

"Look at it this way," Aslan spoke, "If King Damon is stronger than we thought, we should be able to outrun him. We'll be on foot and he'll be in a wagon, we can just run through the trees."

"Besides, as long as I'm around, you know I'll be here to make sure you're in good shape," Aliyah said with a comforting smile.

"She's never looked at me like that before," Dante thought to himself, "What in the hells is going on?"

The ground shook underneath them again, this time even more aggressively, nearly bouncing Dante off the ground. As he sprawled outward quickly to catch himself, he looked around at everyone who remained perfectly calm.

"How is this not bothering any of you?" Dante asked.

"You worry too much, Dante," Faetu dismissed.

"Don't be so skittish," Aslan added. "You act like you've never felt a quake before."

"Everything is perfectly okay, Dante," Aliyah spoke comfortingly.

Dante scrambled to his feet; he was certain something was wrong, but he couldn't prove it. He started looking around at where they were and noticed he had never seen this place before. In the distance, there was a mountain with a waterfall streaming from midway down its slope, with a grass plain between its base and them. They were under a great maple tree that stretched high above them, and Aslan sat perched on one of its branches. Kinomaru leaned back against a large rock that was positioned at the base of the tree, and Faetu sat next to Aliyah at the edge of the hill before it sloped downward toward the plain.

"I don't understand," Dante said as he desperately tried to connect the dots.

But suddenly, there was another tremor. This was the most violent one yet, knocking him off his feet. He was sent into the air and came crashing down to the earth. However, there was no ground beneath him when he fell. It was as though the soil itself parted and allowed Dante to fall inside before closing above him and sealing him within.

Dante tried to claw back up, but he felt nothing as he tumbled into blackness. Then, another tremor, and another, and another. Dante tried his best to see in the blackness, but it was an all-consuming darkness that hid away any light. He tried to open his eyes wider and wider, but it remained a void.

Then, the hardest tremor he had felt finally allowed some light to shine through. He slowly soaked in the sunlight at first, but was almost disgusted by how cold the soil had become. It gave him a shiver as he felt the frigid dirt beneath his cheek. He then felt another bounce, but this time it was accompanied by the faintest sound of clanging metal.

This confused him further, but he slowly soaked up more sunlight to try to get a better view of his surroundings. As his blurry vision started to clear, he felt a sudden rush of pain shoot across his body. His muscles ached, and he felt bruised and battered. The pain was constant and throbbing, but not excruciating.

"What is this? Where am I?" Dante thought to himself as he tried his best to see what was going on. "What happened to me? Am I in Damon's wagon? Where is everyone else?"

As his senses became clearer, he realized the sunlight wasn't from the sun, but instead from a torch just outside of a barred window. The sound of hooves striking stone beat in his ear like a rhythmic drum, which was followed by another tremor that bounced him off the ground slightly.

The tremor revealed itself to be nothing more than bumps in the road as Dante became aware. He did his best to hold still as he tried to process everything that was happening. Bouncing back and forth between dreams and reality was confusing to him.

"So it really did happen," Dante thought. "Aslan is dead. And Kinomaru and Aliyah, are they still alive? And Faetu… Faetu is dead as well. I saw him die right in front of me, and there was nothing I could do about it. Why…? All this talk about becoming King, and he died. How could this happen?
You always said you'd have my back, and you died next to me. You always said I was destined for greatness, and that's why you kept me around, but what did you mean by that? Why did you have to die? And why were you… smiling at me? Why, Faetu?"

Dante's head was reeling in confusion as he tried his best to grasp what was happening. Once he was finally able to get a look around, he quickly froze in position. Nearly touching his knees were a pair of boots belonging to an armed man sitting on a wagon's bench. The man hadn't noticed he was awake yet and appeared to have his eyes locked on something on the opposite side of the wagon.

He took a slow breath to calm himself and try to assess the situation. He could see Damon's crest on the man's armor, so he knew he was in custody, but he had no clue how he ended up in a wagon, or where he was being taken. He knew it wasn't going to be a pleasant destination, so he started looking for a way out.

"I won't be able to just outrun him," Dante realized. "If I take him out, maybe I'll get a better view where I'm at. I'll have to be fast, though, so I can finish off whoever is behind me. Worst case scenario is Damon is behind me, he'll kill me for sure, but that beats wherever he's taking me. But how do I do it?"

He started to look around as unassumingly as possible when he noticed a small dagger tucked into a shallow sheath just above the guard's knee. The weapon looked barely secured, which would make it easy to remove if he tried. However, the man held a sword in his hand, so he would have to react as quickly as possible if he wanted to avoid getting skewered.

"I can't just reach out for it, though; he'll react too quickly," Dante plotted. "I'll just wait for the next bump in the road and then go for it. That should buy me at least an extra second, which will be all I need. If I'm wrong, I guess it won't be my problem anymore."

Dante's heart beat quickly as he nervously waited for the next bump. He was terrified of dying, but even more afraid of what would happen to him if he arrived at his destination. The seconds ticked by slowly, but as sure as the sun rose, the wagon hit another bump on the road.

Despite his fear, Dante moved without hesitation. He jumped up at the first twitch of the wagon beneath him and pounced for the dagger. The man's eyes stretched wide once he realized what was happening, but it was too late for him to react. Dante had already grabbed the blade from his thigh and slammed it into his throat.

Dante quickly jerked the dagger from the man's neck and spun around to slam the weapon into whoever was behind him. King Damon, another guard, it didn't matter. He didn't care who it was; he just wanted them dead so he could leave, but as soon as he twisted around, his hand was grabbed out of the air.

He almost burst into tears as he whipped around and realized who he was looking at. The tip of his blade was inches away from Aliyah's face, and she had a look of panic and fear in her eyes. Kinomaru slowly released Dante's hand from his grasp and sank back in his seat. He looked at Dante as if he had never expected what he had just seen to happen.

"Aliyah? Kinomaru? You're alive!" Dante said quietly, but excitedly.

The wagon hit another bump, and the guard fell from his seat and slammed into the ground. Blood fell from his throat and soaked his clothing beneath his armor, but he wasn't moving.

"Dante, what are you doing?" Aliyah asked.

"I don't know," Dante answered as he tried to figure out what was going on. "Where are we?"

"We were taken captive by Damon, and we're being taken to Angron Prison. But they'll kill us when they find him," Aliyah answered.

"They were going to kill us anyway," Dante said, waving off her worry. "We have to get out of here."

"How? Where are we going to go, Dante?" Aliyah asked, angrily. "We lost. We lost our freedom… and we lost our friends." Tears began to well up in her eyes as she spoke, and she buried her face in her palms and sobbed. "And now, we are going to lose our lives."

"No," Dante barked, doing his best to mask his own worries. "We are going to find a way out of here."

Kinomaru pointed toward the small window on the side of the wagon. The window was barred, so it wasn't an option to get through it, but Dante quickly noticed they were approaching massive walls. He leaned closer to take a peek out of the window and saw they were already at the gate of the prison.

"Damnit," Dante muttered. "If we slip out right now, the guards on the wall will see us."

"I told you, Dante, there's no escaping now. Faetu was sure we could win, and look what happened," Aliyah said as she tried her best to control her grief. "Once they open that door and see their friend dead, we will be joining him."

"And I would rather die fighting than live as a prisoner," Dante stated.

"I don't disagree," Aliyah muttered. "But what choice do we even have?"

"We'll open this door and slip out at the right time," Dante explained. "Once we're out of the wagon, all we have to do is find a way back out of the prison, and we're free."

"You say that like it's easy," Aliyah huffed.

"No, I say it like it's the only choice we have. If Faetu were here, he would say the same thing," Dante preached. He looked Aliyah in the eyes and could see the pain she was in, as well as Kinomaru's. He could feel a lump growing in his throat as his lip quivered slightly, saying, "I'm hurt too. Faetu has always been there for me; he played with me when the other kids laughed. He accepted me when the other kids rejected the strange orphan boy. And Aslan has been like family for years. I'm devastated that they're gone. I want nothing more than for them to be alive, but I can't change anything that happened. However, I can change what hasn't, and that is us dying. We're still here, so we still have to fight."

Kinomaru leaned forward slightly and placed his hand on Dante's shoulder. Dante raised his head to look him in the eyes, and Kinomaru gave him a nod of understanding.

"Thank you, Kinomaru. Despite everything that's happened, I really am glad you two are with me. This would be so much more difficult had I been the only one who survived," Dante muttered. "I don't know what I would do if I were alone; it would probably break me."

Aliyah let out a slow sigh as she could see Dante was hurting too. She leaned over him to get closer to the window and secure a better view of where they were. She decided to help come up with an escape plan rather than give up so easily.

She stood there for a moment before stepping back and saying, "If we time it right, we may be able to slip away between the guards inside. Angron Prison is a massive complex, so it's unlikely to be tightly guarded along all the walkways. We should be able to slip through their defenses, but I doubt it will work for long."

Dante's cheeks were a little flushed as he answered, "Uh, yes, that's what I was thinking. Kinomaru, can you break out of here quietly?"

Kinomaru grabbed the dead guard's leg and pulled his body toward the front of the wagon before he stepped over to the back. He grabbed the door before shaking it a couple of times to test its durability and looked back at Dante as if he were waiting for the signal.

"Right," Dante affirmed. "Let's do this."

Dante peeked out the window and saw the massive gates pass over top of them and begin closing behind them as they traveled within the walls of Angron Prison. He stayed close to the side of the wall to avoid getting spotted by any guards that may be peeking. But once they were inside, the area seemed to clear up quickly.

Winding paths trailed off in every direction, and most of them seemed to travel toward what looked to be a large mine in the distance. A few prisoners were shambling toward the mine, and a few others were shambling back with large stones on their backs. The prisoners were bound in ankle shackles, and all of them appeared emaciated and malnourished.

Dante did a quick scan of the area that he could see and noticed there were no guards in the immediate vicinity. He couldn't tell about the opposite side of the wagon, but he could see a guardhouse in the distance with two other wagons posted in front of it, so he guessed that was their destination.

"It's now or never, guys," Dante said as he took a quick breath.

Kinomaru nodded and slowly pushed against the wagon door. The lock holding the doors together broke easily, but since Kinomaru didn't have to bash the door to break it, the whole event was relatively quiet and undetectable. Kinomaru took a quick peek outside the door before opening it entirely and letting the others go before him.

Dante stepped out quietly and rapidly scanned the area before picking a set of buildings to slip between. Aliyah and Kinomaru followed close behind, and the three of them moved as fast but quietly as they could to get away from the wagon.

They knew better than to try to talk to one another, so Dante communicated with hand signals to wave them on or try to stop them. Once they were between the two buildings, they took a second to survey their surroundings. The structures around them were all made of stone, likely mined by the prisoners, and there was a maze of alleyways running between them. The prison almost looked like a city, with so many pathways and buildings.

Dante was on edge as he looked for a place to go. He could hear people talking all around him and knew one wrong move would spell death for everyone. He looked up to see dusk had just passed, so it was likely time for everything to start winding down for the night, which meant they only needed a place to hide for a few hours before it would be easier to escape.

They kept close to the wall of one of the buildings as they crept down the alleyway. Dante wasn't sure where he was leading everyone, but he wanted to keep moving until he could find something. They passed small open areas and moved from crevice to crevice as he searched for a hiding spot, but nowhere felt safe enough to hide for very long.

Eventually, they stumbled onto an intersection of alleyways and saw the glimmer of a torchlight coming closer to them. Dante immediately started to look for somewhere to go, but each direction was open, with nowhere to hide. He grabbed the handle of an iron door next to him and realized it was unlocked. He pushed it open a little to see that the door led down some stairs, but there were no people on the other side. He waved the three of them in and closed the door behind them just before the guard stepped around the corner.

"That was too close," Dante thought to himself.

He looked further in to see a set of spiral stairs circling downward away from the door. He had no idea where they might lead, but the only choice they had was to find out. He couldn't see back out of the door, and he didn't want to risk opening it again and someone seeing them.

He started to descend the stairs, one foot at a time, as he peeked his head around the corner with each step he took. The stairs always turned out of view quickly, so he was painfully nervous that they would stumble into someone as they walked, but after spinning down what felt like a hundred stairs, they finally reached the bottom.

There was a torchlit hallway that stretched far ahead and seemed to split at the end. The hall looked almost empty except for a few doors scattered down one side of the hall. The doors all looked the same, and they were closed with a wheel that turned and locked them in place.

Dante slowly started to lead them down the hallway as they kept a sharp eye ahead of them. They could hear voices carrying from far into the distance, but didn't see any movement. The torches along the wall were spaced far enough apart to create pockets of darkness, which was comforting but still not enough to hide in.

After they passed the second door, they began to see a torchlight at the end of the hallway growing brighter. They paused for a second to get a better look, but it took minimal time to tell that someone was coming closer. They knew they couldn't stay in the hall, so Dante quickly stepped back and turned the wheel on the door as quietly as possible. The iron bars squeaked slightly as they slid out of their recesses, and the door opened in front of him.

They all stepped inside and closed the door behind them. Kinomaru did his best to twist a bolt that held the wheel in place from the other side. His grip was just strong enough to turn it a quarter of the way back, but not enough to secure the door entirely. Once he did, they stood with their backs against the walls and waited quietly as the light under the door slowly grew brighter.

Eventually, they began to hear footsteps drawing closer with each beat. The torchlight that danced underneath the crack of the doorframe went from a dull glow to nearly bright enough to cast shadows. With each step that echoed off the walls and down the hallway, the sound of chattering metal followed.

Dante took a slow breath, held it briefly, then let it out, slowing his heart rate. He took a firm grip on the dagger he still had and stood ready to attack if he needed to. He looked at Kinomaru and saw that he stood prepared to strike as well.

Time felt as though it was dragging as they waited to see what would happen. The footsteps grew loud enough that they could hear them over the echoes, and the metal chattering grew with it. They were sure whoever was outside had stopped right in front of the door, and their worry skyrocketed as the footsteps ground to a halt.

"Who the hells left this door unlocked?" a voice muttered from the outside.

The bolt holding the wheel began to turn, but it didn't lock the door; instead, it opened. The door swung ajar, but they remained where they were. They hoped whoever opened it would peek inside and leave, but to their dismay, the man stepped inside.

"I brought you your-" the man spoke as he walked into the room, but was abruptly cut short.

Kinomaru grabbed the man by the throat and immediately started to choke him from behind. A loud crashing sound screamed down the halls as the tray of food the man was holding fell to the ground. However, that would be the only sound that escaped the room.

Dante jumped over toward Kinomaru and slammed his dagger into the man's chest, piercing his heart. Kinomaru held onto the man until he felt him stop moving, and then gently laid him down on the ground while Aliyah closed the door. Dante was breathing rapidly, but quickly grabbed the man by his leg and dragged him away from the view of the door. Once he did, the three of them placed themselves back against the walls and waited to see if anyone else was coming.

The silence was deafening as they stared at the door for what felt like an eternity. But they began to relax slightly after some time passed, and they heard no footsteps or saw no light. They still maintained their attention, as they didn't want to be caught off guard, but then they heard something that immediately sent them into a panic.

"That was my dinner," a deep and gravely voice spoke out from deeper in the room.

They immediately snapped their attention to the source of the noise and barely made out a figure kneeling in the center of the room. Dante carefully crouched, grabbed the torch the guard was carrying, and held it up to get a better view. They were surprised to see they hadn't stumbled into some dark, empty room at all.

Kneeling in the center of the room was a man bound in multiple chains. A harness wrapped around his body like a vice that was secured to an iron collar that wrapped around his neck. The chains, fastened at multiple points along his body, were anchored to hooks molded into the stone floor. The man was chained by his neck and torso, and his arms were forced outward and fastened in a way that wouldn't let him bring them closer to himself. His hands were also wrapped in iron gloves that secured at his wrists.

Whoever he was, he was clearly dangerous…

Chapter 7

"Is some of it salvageable?" the man asked again as he stared at the ground in front of him.

"What do you mean?" Dante asked with a shaky voice.

"I mean my meal," the man responded. "Is any of it salvageable?"

Dante looked down at the tray and saw that it was completely smashed. Food was strewn across the floor, and the dishware was shattered.

"No, it's gone," Dante answered.

"I see," the man said with a sigh.

"Who are you?" Aliyah asked. "Why are you here?"

"I could ask you the same thing," the man grunted. "Who breaks into a prison?"

"We didn't break in; we were forced to come here against our will," Dante explained.

"Ah, I take it young Damon sent you here then?" the man asked.

The three of them exchanged glances as the prisoner spoke. They had never heard King Damon referred to as 'young Damon' before, which piqued their curiosity.

"Do you know King Damon?" Aliyah asked.

"We have a history," the prisoner responded.

"Then how did you end up here?" Dante asked again.

"Because I'm a monster," the man answered. "A monster that he fears."

"If he fears you, then we are on the same side," Aliyah said as she slowly started to approach him. "I can take these chains off of you and-"

"No," the man barked. "Leave them."

"Why?" Aliyah asked.

"Because I need to be chained. I'm dangerous," he responded.

"We need dangerous," Aliyah argued.

"Are you sure, Aliyah?" Dante asked. "We don't know anything about this guy."

"Of course I'm sure," Aliyah argued. "King Damon killed our friends, and I don't know of any other way to beat him. He deserves to be punished for all the villages he's destroyed, all the lives he's ruined, for Aslan, and… for Faetu. He says King Damon is afraid of him, which makes him valuable to us."

"You plan to kill young Damon?" the prisoner asked.

"Yes, we tried once already, but we lost. Two of our friends died in the process," Dante answered.

"So let me help you go free, and in return, you help us kill Damon," Aliyah offered.

The man sighed and seemed to ponder on his following words a moment before saying, "I would love to get my hands on young Damon. It would only be fitting for what he has put me through, but I cannot be free of these chains unless I am certain my bloodlust will be contained."

"We can help you with that," Aliyah offered.

The man picked up his head for the first time in the conversation and looked up at Aliyah. He admired her youthful beauty and warm expression, and could see in her eyes that she meant what she said. She was slightly taken aback by the deep red tint of his eyes, filled with malice.

"Please, sir, we need all the help we can get," Aliyah asked, ignoring her initial worry.

"Listen, what you are asking is a lot more than you think, and a lot more dangerous than you think. Before I agree to anything that involves me being free of these bindings, I need all of you to understand who I am and what I've done," the man offered.

"We're listening," Aliyah agreed.

"Young Damon and I have a long history together. I trained him when he was a small boy, and I raised him on the battlefield. His father was a war general in the previous King's army, and young Damon wanted to follow in his father's footsteps.

As young Damon grew, so did his power, as well as his ruthlessness. He had murdered dozens of men by the time he was fourteen, and he seemed unbothered by it. Now, killing has never been a problem for me or anyone else in the war party, but it was uncommon for someone so young to be so comfortable with it.

I continued to train young Damon, day in and day out, and by the time he was a man, his power exceeded my own. He had learned to control the elements around him as if they were extensions of his own body. He would walk into battle without a care in the world as people struggled to lay a single scratch on him," the prisoner explained.

"I noticed that too," Dante blurted. "When I tried to strike him, I could only barely inch my blade closer to him, even with all my strength."

"That's because he uses the air around him and pushes it outward, creating a barrier to protect him that is nearly impossible to cut through," the prisoner explained. "He used that barrier to intimidate and demoralize his enemies, laying waste to entire armies nearly alone. By now, I would guess his kill count rivals my own.

We destroyed anyone who opposed our King, and there were many who tried, but we never faltered. Our war party was especially effective at killing, as if it were second nature to us. We kept the King safe and his borders secure.

However, killing alone was not enough to satisfy young Damon. He wanted more power, more land, and more riches. His greed was boundless, and his ruthlessness was unmatched. He and I would step away from the front lines of battle to infiltrate deep into enemy territory and destroy them from the inside out. Soldiers or civilians, it didn't matter. At the end of the day, dead people could never help their country, so we killed them all. I can't even count the number of people I've slain, the number of houses burned, or the number of corpses cremated in the streets. It has to be tens of thousands."

"You're a monster," Dante muttered.

"I have been saying that," the prisoner growled. "You think I'm not aware of the sins of my actions? You think I haven't had YEARS to sit here and cycle through the countless faces of those I've killed for fun? If you think that, you haven't been listening. I know I'm a monster, and a monster I will remain until I draw my final breath. Whether that be at the hands of someone stronger than me or at the fate of the god of time."

"But King Damon is no different. He still kills anyone who opposes him without question and without care. If you are the monster you say you are, then why are you bound in chains and not still sitting beside him?" Aliyah asked.

"Because he's afraid of me," the man muttered. "We had been killing Kingdoms from the inside out for years when his father first learned about what we were doing. I was lashed for my insolence, while young Damon was only scolded. We were forbidden from ever crossing into enemy borders again.

Young Damon was furious at this order, but our hands were tied, and we could no longer conduct our missions in private. I began to thirst for battle, but the bordering Kingdoms had entered into peace agreements, and the wars along the borders were coming to an end. There was no longer a need for machines of war like us.

The King came to meet with young Damon's father to discuss the future of his company. There were a few of us in attendance, and we were informed that the Kingdom no longer needed our expertise on the borders and that he would rather we get cozy in the castle until we retired.

This was an infuriating idea, and young Damon was outspokenly against it. He recommended we take the fight to our enemies and spread the borders of our Kingdom far and wide. The King rightfully admonished young Damon, but this would only fuel the fire.

Young Damon grew angry and violent, drawing his blade. His father tried to stop him, but nothing was working. He lunged toward the King and plunged his blade into the King's heart, all while the guards around him tried desperately to stop him. But none of their attacks could penetrate the barrier, and they were helpless as they watched their King die before them.

His father tried to grab him, but young Damon turned on him as well, slicing his blade across his throat before turning his attention toward the rest of the people around him. He stared everyone down and coldly told them to stand and face him if they felt he was wrong. No one else did. From that day forward, young Damon proclaimed himself the King.

I don't know much about what happened since then. I imagine he struggled to seize control of the villages and towns already in the Kingdom; they were loyal to the previous King and would likely need to be forced into submission under a new rule. But it has been years since then, I imagine he has since expanded and grown his borders."

"So Damon truly is a madman," Dante muttered, "Killing his own father in cold blood."

"That doesn't explain how you ended up here, though," Aliyah noted aloud.

"After he killed the King and his father, young Damon came to me and asked me what I thought of his actions. I was honest when I told him he was wrong. His response has been with me ever since. He said, 'We are born to kill. It's what we're good at, it's what we're known for, and it's what fuels us. We thrive off killing, and without bloodshed, we are nothing.

Taking another life in the palm of our hands is the only thing that keeps men like us alive. This disposition is what makes us so good at what we do, and what makes us so dangerous to people who disagree with us. You disagree with me, old friend. I cannot have someone with murder in their souls walking alongside me, but I also cannot allow such a dear friend to die.'

I should have killed him then; I could have saved myself a lifetime of solitude and anguish. I could have saved the Kingdom from his rule, but I didn't; I froze. After that, he locked me away. I don't know how long I've been in this hole. It's been decades since I've seen the light of the sun, and all I can see are the faces of those I've killed playing on repeat. I am the monster he says I am. I will never be satisfied unless I'm killing. My blood lust is as great as it's ever been. I miss the remarkable feeling, but I don't want to end another life. The only person I want to kill is young Damon, then my wrongs will be righted. My story can come to an end," the prisoner elaborated.

"But if no one can get through the barrier of his, why lock you away?" Dante asked.

"Because the barrier fails when put against extreme heat," the prisoner explained. "My flames burn unlike any other."

"That is why he avoided all of Faetu's attacks but none of mine," Dante thought to himself. Faetu was the perfect counter for him."

"With that being explained, with the evil of my sins brought to light, and the murderous intent in my soul on full display, do you still want my help?" the man asked. "I am no saint, no, far from it. I am a devil, and the only thing I am good at is killing. Releasing me from these bonds doesn't change that; it only allows me to continue."

"I am sure," Aliyah claimed. "King Damon needs to pay for what he's done, and we could use your help in doing it."

"If you can take me to young Damon, I will end his life. It is the least I can do," the man agreed.

"Are we sure we're doing the right thing here?" Dante asked. "If a man like Damon fears him, shouldn't we as well? How do we know he won't start killing like Damon?"

"We don't," Aliyah answered. "But if he can help us kill King Damon, then we can deal with the rest of it afterward. After what happened, I don't care if we're releasing another monster into the world. As long as this monster will help us kill the other, then it's a risk I'm willing to take."

"Okay, if you're sure, I won't argue the point anymore," Dante ceded. He looked at the prisoner and said, "We'll be watching every move you make. Even if it costs my life, I will cut you down if you raise a hand to an innocent person."

The prisoner looked him directly in the eyes; his crimson-tinted irises felt like they pierced his skin and peered into his soul. The glare was unnerving and menacing, but his facial expression was blank and unfeeling. The prisoner had an aura that matched the sinister definition of a devil.

"I hope you do," the prisoner said as he looked Dante in his eyes.

Aliyah glanced over toward Kinomaru and gave him a nod, asking for his help in breaking the chains around the man's body. Kinomaru walked over to them and grabbed hold of one of the anchors in the stone floor. He planted his feet and pulled as hard as he could.

The sound of shifting rock echoed off the walls before the anchor eventually ripped from the floor. Now that one of the man's arms was free, Kinomaru was able to get a better angle on the shackles around him. Piece by piece, he grabbed and snapped the various holds and bindings around the man's body. He pulled the iron gloves apart and ripped the harness into pieces, freeing the prisoner of all of his bindings except for the collar.

The man stood to his feet slowly and groaned as he stretched his limbs. His body was covered in scars, his skin was callused where the shackles wrapped around him, and his body appeared aged and weathered. He was lean, but still surprisingly muscular after spending years in captivity. He was far from Kinomaru's size but was larger than Dante. He grunted as he finished his stretch and began walking toward the guard Dante had killed. Kinomaru and Dante were skeptical and kept their guard up.

"That may have been easier if you used this," the man said as he reached down and grabbed a key from the guard's waist.

He unlocked the collar around his neck and dropped it to the ground before he rubbed the wound around his throat where the collar had cut into his skin for years. His body had been permanently changed by the chains over time, giving him a constant reminder of his captivity.

"I really hope we don't regret this," Dante thought. "I can feel the bloodlust radiating from this man, but if he is as strong as he says he is, then maybe we can kill Damon after all. We can avenge Faetu and put an end to this nightmare."

The man reached down and picked up the guard's corpse by the collar of his armor. He started unfastening the armor from the guard's body, removing it piece by piece, slowly taking apart the gear and dropping it to the ground. Once he removed all of the armor, he began to put the pieces on himself. It took some time, but eventually he put all the armor on and turned to face the rest of the group.

Dante stood in front of Aliyah, still wielding the dagger in his hand, and asked, "You never told us your name. What is it?"

"My name?" the man asked rhetorically, "My name is Diabhal. Captain of the Ghosts of War, and wielder of the black flame."

Daibhal held his hand in front of him with his palm upward. It suddenly burst into flames, but they were unlike anything they had seen before. The flames on his hand were as black as a moonless night, yet radiated an ominous energy that could be felt from across the room.

"With this flame, I will put young Damon to rest and atone for the sins my hand played in creating that monster," Daibhal muttered as he looked at the fire. Sadness filled his eyes as he watched the flame dancing at the tips of his fingers, and he spoke to himself, "It has been such a long time."

Chapter 8

"Do you know of a way out of here?" Dante asked.

"You know more about what's beyond that door than I do. I've lived in this room for longer than I care to remember. But getting out won't be a problem," Diabhal answered.

"Why won't it?" Aliyah asked.

"Because we will kill whoever tries to stop us," Diabhal answered.

"What makes you so confident?" Dante asked.

"I'm starting to wonder if you struggle to listen," Diabhal growled. "Killing is my specialty. If helpless fools present themselves to me on a silver platter, I will eat."

Dante swallowed a lump in his throat as Diabhal's malice was palpable. He could tell there were no lies in his words, that he planned on killing anyone who stood in the way. It was like the man was truly a devil.

"Then follow me," Dante said. "We can leave the way we came."

Dante pulled the door open and slowly stuck his head out to see if anyone was coming. However, there were no guards in the immediate hallway, so they started back toward the stairs they had come from.

Kinomaru made sure to walk at the back of the group to keep an eye on Diabhal. Despite his openness and honesty,

Kinomaru didn't seem to trust him, or he was being cautious. Aliyah walked just behind Dante, and the four calmly but quickly made their way down the hall and back toward the spiral stairs.

Once they reached the stairs, they could hear voices farther up. Dante immediately hugged the wall to stay as out of sight as possible, and everyone but Diabhal did the same. Dante looked at him in confusion but didn't say a word. Instead, he waited patiently as the footsteps grew louder and the speech became clearer.

Two guards walked down the stairs, talking to one another. They were talking about an open wagon with a dead guard inside, and that if they came down into the tunnels, they could avoid getting tasked to the search party. They laughed at how genius their plan was until they finally descended far enough to see Diabhal standing on the staircase.

Both men scrambled for their weapons as soon as they saw him, but they weren't fast enough. They thought they were getting away from trouble, but they accidentally stumbled right into it. Dante jumped from around the corner and slammed his dagger into one of their throats while Diabhal grabbed the other by the face. With his hand over the guard's mouth, he blasted a stream of black flame that immediately melted the man's flesh until the flame sputtered out of the back of his head. The heat was so intense that it boiled and evaporated the blood before it could pour. Within seconds, both guards were dead, and the smell of burning flesh assaulted their noses.

"You'll get used to the stench after a while," Diabhal muttered.

Dante handed his dagger back to Aliyah before reaching down and grabbing a longsword from one of the guards; Diabhal grabbed the other. Dante could see the sadness in his eyes, but his expression was apathetic. He seemed to find a solemn sense of pain from what he had just done.

"Let's move," Dante suggested.

Diabhal nodded and motioned for Dante to lead the way, and they continued to climb the stairs until they finally reached the door. Dante slowly opened the door once again and was pleased to see no one was waiting for them on the other side.

"We likely have a couple of minutes at best before this place is swarming with guards," Dante thought. "The more people we run into, the more likely we are to set the prison on high alert. In fact, I don't see a way for us to get out of here without a fight."

Dante worried to himself in silence as he led the group. He retraced his steps as best as he could, but they took quite a few turns on their way into hiding, so it was difficult for him to remember exactly where they came from.

They took turn after turn, slowly making their way closer to the gate of the prison, when the silence was abruptly replaced by chaos. A horn blew so loud that it rattled their chest cavities, and the horn was followed by sounds of screaming and shouting in the distance. At first, they weren't sure what all the screaming was about, but eventually they started to hear the yelling more clearly.

"PRISONER ONE HAS ESCAPED! ALL HANDS REPORT!" multiple people started yelling from all corners of the prison.

"Prisoner one?" Aliyah asked quietly.

"Yes, this prison was built around me," Diabhal explained. "There is no escaping without a fight now."

Kinomaru began looking around for something to use as a weapon, but found nothing but stone walls and dirt. Diabhal saw him searching and shook his head.

"There is no need for that right now. It's me they're after, just stand back," Diabhal ordered.

A black flame shot down the edge of the sword Diabhal was holding, wrapped around the tip, and then shot back up the other side, creating a fine flame that just danced along the edges of the weapon. Dante was stunned to see that the immense heat from the flame wasn't melting the weapon immediately, but then he noticed a tiny buffer zone between the flame and the blade.

"Stay here. I will return momentarily," Diabhal said.

The three of them were hesitant to agree, but nodded and pressed themselves against a wall. They felt like children as Diabhal walked away, casually approaching the source of all the noise. They watched as he disappeared around the corner, and a minute later, the sounds of screaming and battle began to ring through the air.

"What is going on?" Dante wondered. "Is he really going to fight all of them by himself? What if he dies? How would we get away then?" He looked back at the others and asked, "Should we go help him?"

"What if we just get in the way?" Aliyah asked.

"And what if he dies and we have no choice but to escape without him. It's been decades since he's been free; he might be rusty," Dante argued.

"You might be right," Aliyah agreed. "Let's go look."

Dante gripped his sword and slowly made his way toward the source of the fighting. The screaming was ear-curling, and they could hear the sound of steel meeting flesh with more clarity the closer they walked. Before they found Diabhal, they had already seen a trail of bodies leading them to where they wanted to go. Eventually, they reached the edge of the final building, and Dante peeked his head around the corner to see what was happening; he was stunned at what he saw.

Diabhal moved like a monster. He was incredibly fast and looked like he was designed to kill. Each attack that came his way wasn't just blocked; they were redirected and used to his advantage. There were no wasted motions in his movements, and with each swing of his sword, another life was taken.

"How does one man do all of this?" Dante muttered.

Diabhal ducked under the swing of a blade as he sliced his own across the guard's chest. His sword melted through the steel and easily dug its way in and back out of the guard's body, flaying him open and leaving him to bleed out. Diabhal leaned out of the way of a bolt of lightning magic that streaked across the battlefield, shot a quick plume of black flames that melted an arrow intended for his head, sliced his blade into an incoming strike from a sword that cut the blade in half, decapitated the guard who tried to tried to cut him, grabbed the broken blade out of the air, covered it in flames, and threw it at another guard with enough force to tunnel through his heart.

"Have we made a mistake?" Dante worried as he saw the potential for damage this one prisoner was capable of.

Without leaving cover, Dante watched Diabhal move like water in a bottle. He was untouchable as countless guards tried their best to bring him down, but all of them failed. One by one, each guard was cut down. His sword melted through their bodies, his flames scorched their flesh, and his expression never shifted. He killed dozens of men until the only ones left were fleeing for their lives. Diabhal didn't chase them. Instead, he let them retreat deeper into the prison while he turned and started walking toward the gate.

When Diabhal turned around, Dante could see agony in his eyes. He looked as though he was about to burst into tears, but the sinister aura around him was as threatening as ever. If anything, it was more noticeable than before, which was alarming.

"Are you worried they will come back?" Dante asked.

"No, they won't," Diabhal answered with certainty. "But this fight isn't finished."

Dante nodded in acknowledgement, and they all started to approach the gate. Aliyah snagged a bow from one of the dead guards, and Kinomaru snapped a wooden beam from an awning to use as a makeshift club. They figured they would need some weapons for the battle to come, and had no intention of being helpless if they could avoid it. There was no point in trying to sneak, as the entire prison was on high alert. It would be impossible for them to get out without being spotted, so they walked toward the gate down the main road.

Before they reached the gate, they could see a row of people standing on the wall waiting for them. There were even more people standing in a line formation in front of the closed gate, acting as a last line of defense to stop Diabhal from escaping. They continued to walk until Diabhal stopped no more than a hundred feet from the gate.

"Prisoner one," a man from the top of the gate shouted. "What do you think you're doing?"

"I will only say this once, warden. Open the gate and stand aside. I do not wish to make your wives widows," Diabhal threatened.

The warden laughed loudly, but it was clear the threat seeped into the hearts of many of the guards, as fear sat in their eyes and their hands trembled.

"You can't hope to take all of us with nothing more than a few inexperienced kids," the warden shouted.

"I can kill you all alone, and you know that. All of you know that, so leave now if you wish to go home tonight," Diabhal warned.

Many of the guards started chattering among themselves as they looked around at everyone else. It was like dozens of them were waiting on someone else to make the first move. Finally, one of the guards on the ground level dropped his sword and shield and began walking away.

"I don't want to die today," the guard shouted before his walk escalated to running.

Anger resonated on the warden's face as he grabbed a crossbow from one of the men next to him and fired at the fleeing guard. The bolt slammed into the back of his neck, and the guard fell to the ground before sliding to a halt.

"Is anyone else feeling like a coward today? No? Good," the warden barked. "Now, Diabhal, you know King Damon doesn't want to see you harmed, but if you leave us no choice, we will gladly kill you."

Diabhal let out a slow sigh as he closed his eyes and let his head rock back. He looked almost filled with regret and frustration.

"Ready!" the warden shouted as everyone along the top wall aimed their crossbows, "Aim!"

"Don't move," Diabhal mumbled as he opened his eyes and looked back toward the warden.

"FIRE!" the warden shouted as two dozen bolts came flying toward the group.

Diabhal threw his hand forward and matched the volley of bolts with a firestorm of cataclysmic proportions. The plume of flames engulfed the bolts, melting them nearly instantly before it stretched up to where the warden stood. All they could hear were the screams of over a dozen men as they sprinted along the wall, trying desperately to put out the flames that wrapped around them, but eventually they all perished. The warden never had the chance to scream; his body melted almost immediately.

"There's still more," Aliyah shouted as she drew her bow and fired an arrow, plunging it into the neck of one of the archers along the wall. "I'll deal with them; you all take care of the others."

The black flames danced all along the top of the wall as they burned the very stone it was constructed with. The flames were disorienting and burned so hot that they obscured the view of the archers who remained. Aliyah took her time to line up her shots, but she could hear the guards charging the rest of the group. She wanted to help them deal with everyone at the bottom, so she started to pick her targets as quickly as possible, landing every shot she loosed, and eliminating another enemy with every arrow.

Diabhal stared down the group that approached from below. There were twenty people, each armed with a longsword and shield. All of them were veteran guards, and many of them were faces he had grown used to seeing. He analyzed their formation, assessed their morale, and started to pick apart their weaknesses before they closed the distance. Kinomaru and Dante stood on either side of him, ready to attack when he did.

"If you two want to make it out of this alive, don't try to be a hero. Pick your targets, and only swing after they do. The key to victory isn't being better than your enemy, it's being smarter. Watch their shoulders, that's the first thing that moves. Their shoulders will tell you where and how they will swing their weapons, and then you prepare to parry and counter. Do this, and you might live. Master this and you'll never lose," Diabhal explained.

"I understand," Dante agreed.

Once the guards were twenty feet away, Daibhal blasted a quick plume of flame at the man in the center. The attack was too quick to dodge, and the man was consumed by fire immediately. This disoriented the charge and slowed any momentum they had built, allowing Diabhal and the others a chance to strike.

Dante stepped to the side and lunged forward at the first person that came within range. He plunged his sword into the guard's abdomen and ducked underneath a wild swing meant for his head. He lifted a powerful uppercut that smashed into the guard's chin and followed the attack by kicking him in the chest to remove his sword from his body. The guard fell to the ground in a heap.

Dante looked over and could see Diabhal had already killed three men and was swinging for a fourth. Just past that, he could see Kinomaru slamming the wooden club down into the skull of another guard, which was sure to shatter his brain. Dante was astounded at how quickly either of them was able to eliminate their foes. He felt like he was always lagging behind. Even at such a distance, Aliyah was able to dispatch multiple enemies with her bow. He felt weak, but didn't have any time to dwell on his insecurities.

An arrow whizzed past his head and barely cut into his ear as he leaned to avoid it. He then threw his sword up to block a downward strike from a guard who charged at him. After the block, he felt a powerful elbow strike him in the nose, clouding his vision and throwing his senses for a loop, but he did his best to focus on the man in front of him.

"Watch the shoulders," Dante thought as he tried his best to pay attention, but it didn't seem to help. He quickly swayed to the side to avoid another downward strike and then jumped back to avoid a horizontal slash aimed at his neck. "This isn't helping at all."

Dante swiped his blade to parry a thrusting attack, then used the momentum to carry his blade upward and sliced it diagonally across the guard's body, slamming into the weak point at the guard's neck, and cutting him open.

"That's two," Dante thought to himself as he watched a different guard fall from the top of the gate and slam into the stone below with a thud.

He quickly stepped forward to catch a third man off guard and tried to thrust his sword into the guard's neck as well. The guard leaned to avoid the strike and tried to bring his blade over and down onto Dante's head, but his strike was evaded as well. Dante watched the blade slam into the ground and used the opening to kick the guard in the knee. The guard screamed out in pain as his leg folded backward, snapping in half the wrong direction.

"I'm sorry," Dante muttered as he quickly slashed his blade across the man's neck to end his suffering. "And that's three."

He took a deep breath as he was already feeling the stress of the fight, but when he looked up, he was dumbfounded. The rest of the guards were dead or dying as Kinomaru slammed his club into the side of another guard's head, caving in the helmet and dropping the man immediately. Diabhal slammed his blade through the abdomen of another guard, cutting through his body with ease and splitting the man in two. He then looked back at Aliyah to see her scanning the top of the gate, looking for another target, but there were no more.

"How did they do this that fast?" Dante wondered in amazement as he began counting the bodies. "There were at least six archers along the top of the wall, and eleven men bore the burn wounds from Diabhal's blade. There are six men in a pile near Kinomaru, and I only killed three? What am I doing wrong?"

"That should be the last of them, Diabhal said as he released the flames on his blade. He looked over at Kinomaru and said, "You fight well for a man of your size. Where do you hail from?"

Kinomaru just looked at him, then over at Dante, who chimed in, saying, "He doesn't speak."

"He doesn't?" Diabhal asked.

"No, he's never said a word to anyone," Dante answered. "But he gets easier to read the longer you're around him."

"How long ago did you meet him?" Diabhal asked.

"He walked into town about ten years ago; he's been with us ever since," Dante answered. "Why do you ask?"

"Because I once knew of a people called the Idrasi. They were powerful people who could harness incredible strength through speech. Their powers had been passed down through generations of their ancestry. They were unconquerable and incredibly effective in battle. Your friend resembles them, but they are the opposite of silent," Diabhal explained. "I had heard something bad had happened to them, though. I thought I might get some answers."

Dante looked over at Kinomaru, who had a smile on his face as usual, before saying, "Well, I don't know if Kinomaru is part of these Idrasi you talk about, but he has always been incredibly strong without speaking. He has helped me more times than I care to admit, and luckily, he won't admit it either."

Diabhal looked over at Kinomaru one last time before turning his attention back to the gate and saying, "Let's go, we need to get away from this place before more reinforcements arrive. Once young Damon realizes I have escaped, he will likely go into hiding."

"Do you know where?" Aliyah asked.

"Maybe," Diabhal answered. "But we must not be too hasty."

"So what's the plan?" Dante asked.

"I want to go back to Faetu and Aslan," Aliyah blurted. "They deserve a proper burial, and no one else is going to give it to them."

"How far is this?" Diabhal asked.

"It's not too far," Aliyah answered. "A day's travel at most, to the west."

"Then let's leave," Diabhal agreed as he started walking toward the gate. "I will open the way."

They watched as Diabhal walked over to the gate and looked up and down the thick iron bars. He placed his hand on one of the bars and started to melt it under the intense heat of his flames. Once the bar melted through, he grabbed another and repeated the process. He did this over and over until he broke enough bars to create a doorway large enough for them to fit through, and stepped out of the prison for the first time in over twenty years.

"If you could melt metal like this, why did you remain in captivity?" Aliyah asked.

"The chains minding me were laced with magic suppression, stopping me from being able to harness any of my power," Diabhal answered.

"I'm sorry you had to go through that," Aliyah said comfortingly.

Diabhal ignored her and muttered, "I'm not."

"Let's go get our friends," Dante said quietly as he gave Kinomaru a pat on the back.

They filed out of the makeshift doorway and out onto the road before Dante started to lead them back to the place where Faetu and Aslan's lives were taken. They were still sore from their battles, mentally exhausted from grief, and doing their best to roll with what life had thrown at them. The night sky was filled with stars above their heads, which was at least a slight distraction from their worries.

Despite their tiredness, they pressed onward throughout the night. They used the darkness to travel with less worry, and step by step, they created more distance between them and the prison they had just escaped. After a couple of hours, the adrenaline of battle wore off, and their fatigue began to catch up with them, but they continued walking nonetheless.

Aliyah tried to break the silence by asking Diabhal a question, "So, have you thought about what you will do once we kill King Damon?"

"I don't want to make small talk," Diabhal grunted. "We are not friends, and the sooner you three see me for the monster I am, the easier this whole process will become for you."

"But anyone who is willing to fight for the greater good can't be a monster," Aliyah disagreed.

"What about someone who has slain countless families in cold blood while they begged for their lives? Or what about someone who found joy in ripping fathers from their children, or husbands from their wives, and killing them in cold blood just to send a message to the next generation that would eventually replace my enemies? Can someone who has done that be anything other than a monster?" Diabhal asked.

"Well, I don't know," Aliyah asked.

"I do," Diabhal answered. "I would sooner kill you than become your friend. I am willing to help only because I want to right a personal wrong, and then I want to be done with all of this. I am not doing anything for the greater good, I am only seeking my own personal closure. You all need to realize this sooner rather than later."

"I see," Aliyah noted aloud, falling back a little bit to create a little distance between her and Diabhal. She leaned in close and whispered to Dante, "That guy scares me."

Dante felt the warmth of her breath on his neck as she spoke, and had a cold chill run down his spine. Even if it wasn't romantic, he enjoyed any reason he had to be close to Aliyah. If their circumstances were different, he may have said something in that moment, but it wasn't the time or the place.

"Yeah, me too," Dante agreed with a quiet whisper.

They continued their persistent walking, not slowing down or stopping for anything. It was daybreak before they drew closer to their destination, and their legs were barely keeping their bodies upright. Diabhal seemed unbothered by the walk, especially considering he hadn't walked around in so long. The fact that he retained incredible physical fitness was baffling to Dante, as it shouldn't have been possible.

Not long after daybreak, they rounded a corner and found themselves just up the road from where they lost so much. They could see the bodies of their friends in the distance, and a lump grew in their throats. No matter how much they prepared, they weren't ready to face the result of their defeat.

Chapter 9

The final approach toward their friends was devastatingly difficult. Within minutes of rounding the final corner, they found themselves standing above the bodies of their friends. Tears welled up in all of their eyes except for Diabhal. No matter how much they thought they were ready to see them, the bodies immediately ripped at their hearts and broke them down. Tears fell down Dante's cheeks, Aliyah sobbed quietly, and even Kinomaru had tears well up in his eyes. It was a painful time for all of them.

Dante walked over to Faetu and fell to his knees. He grabbed his severed head and placed it back on his neck as his lip quivered and he failed to fight back tears. He couldn't believe he was gone, and being tired only made the grief that much worse.

"Faetu," Dante whispered. "Why?"

Kinomaru placed his hand on Dante's shoulder and nodded in understanding and to comfort him. He pointed over to a grassy area, just off the path, and Dante knew what he meant.

"I'll see if I can find something to dig with," Dante sighed.

Diabhal walked over to a nearby tree and sat down to rest his head back against the trunk. They knew he wasn't going to help them dig graves, and they felt it was for the best anyway. They also guessed that asking would only lead to problems, so they kept their distance.

They used whatever they could get their hands on to dig. Sticks, swords, and even their bare hands were used to pull the earth away and dig deeper into the soil. Luckily for them, the recent rains loosened the dirt enough to make digging easier, but not so much that it became a muddy endeavour. It took some time, but after about an hour of digging, they had a grave dug for each of their lost companions.

Kinomaru walked over to Aslan and grabbed his body. He laid a piece of cloth over his face to cover the wound before he stepped down into the grave to lay him inside. He crossed his arms over his chest and placed both of his swords in the grave with him. He climbed out of the grave and repeated the process for Faetu's body.

Once both of their friends were laid to rest in the graves, they started to push and scoop the soil back into the holes. The silence was heavy as they filled the graves scoop by scoop, slowly covering their friends with dirt, knowing this would be the last time they would see them. Tears were shed and mixed with the dirt that would fill the grave, but eventually the deed was done.

The three of them stood over the graves as they tried to keep themselves composed. They had spent a long time crying on and off, and the grief was wearing them down slowly. They looked around at one another, waiting to see if anyone wanted to say something, when Aliyah spoke up.

"Aslan gave his life to save mine. The look on his face just before he died is burned into the deepest parts of my mind, and I can't shake it. I hate it," she said suddenly. "Why would he do that? Why would he give up everything for me?"

"Because he cared about you," Dante answered. "He cared about all of us. Despite his dismissive personality, Aslan was a kind man. He wanted what was best for all of us and found joy in being around us, especially you and Faetu. He was always there to crack a joke if things grew too serious, but he was just as quick to raise a weapon at our side."

"And Faetu…" Aliyah said as she covered her mouth and fought back her sobbing. "I loved him dearly, even if he didn't feel the same. I never saw a future without him in it. He seemed invincible and unshakeable. I don't understand why it had to end like this."

"Faetu was the strongest of us all," Dante agreed. "As much as I hate to admit it, Damon said it best. He is everything I am and more. I always walked in his shadow, hoping to be more like him someday. He helped me through the lowest points in my life, and was always there with a smile to guide me back up." Dante wiped a tear from his cheek as he took a shaky breath in and let it out slowly. "I will miss them both so much."

Kinomaru placed his hand on Dante's shoulder again and bowed his head. Dante bowed his head as well and put his arm around Aliyah's shoulders. The three of them stood arm in arm, observing a moment of silence and comforting one another in their grief. Having each other didn't stop the pain, but it made living with it a little easier.

"Damon will pay for this with his life," Dante muttered as a tear fell from his nose. "I stake my own life on it."

They stood there a little longer, riding a roller coaster of grief. The pain acted like the tides of the ocean, growing and fading with each passing moment. But the grief crashed like a tsunami as it tore through their hearts and left them feeling painfully helpless. They wanted so desperately to go back and do things differently, but they couldn't, and living with the pain was the seemingly impossible reality that they were forced to live with.

"Is it your first time losing allies?" Diabhal interrupted suddenly.

"They weren't just allies, they were our closest friends. But yes, it's the first time we've lost people this way," Dante answered.

"You learn to ignore the pain," Diabhal stated.

"I don't want to," Aliyah blurted. "You may be okay with having no ties or bonds to people, but I'm not like you. We love our people, and any loss is devastating, especially one so close to our hearts. So no, I won't learn to ignore the pain, because the pain is a reminder of just how great the love was that was lost."

"Living life like that will lead you to nothing more than a perpetual cycle of grief," Diabhal dismissed.

"If that's how it has to be, then so be it," Dante argued.

Diabhal huffed and shook his head before asking, "What do you know about young Damon's plans?"

"We know he is planning an invasion of Blackhold, and that he is pursuing a dragon named Kavronax," Aliyah answered.

"Kavronax?" Diabhal asked. "Kavronax the Vile?"

"I guess? I don't know, all I know is it's a dragon named Kavronax," Aliyah answered.

"If he is after Kavronax, he is likely on a warpath. But why is he going after such an incredibly powerful dragon?" Diabhal pondered aloud. "And he has plans to take Blackhold as well?"

"Yes, we were able to learn a decent amount of his plans, but still only basic knowledge. We know he plans to take Blackhold by force sometime in the next year, and that he plans on leading his army farther south to pursue Kavronax and kill him," Dante explained.

"If he is chasing Kavronax, it isn't to simply kill him," Diabhal explained. "If he is after Kavronx, it is to harness his power and grow his own. If he consumes Kavronax's power, he will become unstoppable. We have to get to him before then."

"Okay, but we don't know where he is," Dante stated.

"I may," Diabhal said. "There is a castle on the southern border of the empire, one that has been there for generations. It is where the Ghosts of War used to call home. If he is operating on the southern border of the Kingdom, he is sure to be there."

"Then why don't we go there and kill him?" Dante suggested.

"We will, but first, I need to know everything you know about young Damon. I need anything you can tell me about what has happened over the last twenty years. If I can piece together enough, I may be able to answer some of my own questions," Diabhal requested.

"Okay, but please let us finish here first," Dante agreed.

Diabhal paused for a moment before he turned to walk back over to his tree. The rest of the group took a little more time to pay their respects to their fallen friends in silence.

"Faetu, what am I supposed to do?" Dante thought to himself. "It feels like Aliyah and Kinomaru are looking at me to lead them through this, and I don't know how. I'm scared, Faetu. I'm not you, and I am not fit to be a leader. If I could trade my life for yours, I would. You always had a plan, and your confidence was calming to the rest of us.
I know you have been telling me I have some sort of greatness, but where? How do I bring it out? How can I use it, Faetu? If there is greatness inside of me, why can't I find it? All I can find in me is fear, and now I'm even more afraid of losing someone else. If you can hear my thoughts, Faetu, please help me."

After a few minutes had passed, Kinomaru stepped away from the graves and walked over to his hammer. He dusted the dirt off the weapon and placed it on his back in its holster. Aliyah did the same for her bow, tossing the lesser bow to the side that she had looted from the guards.

Dante was the last to walk away. Somewhere deep down, he felt like walking away was sealing the fate of his friends. A small part of him clung to the idea that this tragedy could be undone, hopelessly wishing for them to burst forth from the dirt as if it were all a big joke. He knew it was impossible, but that didn't make it any easier to walk away.

Eventually, Dante took a step back from the graves and walked over to grab his sword. He knelt, brushed the dirt off of it as well, and looked at the blade for a while. He could see Kinomaru standing just off to the side of him, patiently waiting for him to join them.

"You know, Faetu gave me this sword," Dante said to Kinomaru. "He said it was his father's sword, but he couldn't bring himself to wield it. He had the smith embed this jewel into the pommel; it was from Father Edward's ring. This sword means a lot to me, even if it is a little weathered with age. This blade will taste Damon's blood, for everyone we've lost."

Kinomaru gave Dante a pat on the back and then offered his hand to help him to his feet. Dante took the offer and was easily pulled up.

"Thank you, Kinomaru. You've always been there if I needed to talk. I really do appreciate that," Dante said.

Kinomaru smiled at him, as he always had, and the two regrouped with Diabhal and Aliyah. Once they gathered, they walked a little farther to find a place to set up a small campsite for the day. They planned to stay there until nightfall to get some much-needed rest, but didn't want to be near the road in case they were found unexpectedly.

Once they found a spot to settle in, they used the supplies they gathered from what remained of their packs and settled in. They placed some mats down to sleep on and prepared a small campfire to warm the rations they had stored away.

Once they had eaten their meal, Diabhal looked at them and said, "Now that we're comfortable, tell me everything."

Dante and Aliyah spent the next hour explaining everything they could recall about King Damon, his motives, his plans, and the history of the world around them. They tried to explain anything that might help them plan their next move, as well as anything else they thought might be important.

"And that is pretty much anything I can think of," Dante concluded.

"Then we need to travel south, to Stormhelm Castle," Diabhal stated.

"What is Stormhelm Castle?" Aliyah asked.

"A forgotten relic of our history" Diabhal answered. "It was the home of the Ghosts of War. It's west of Huskberg and south of Angelwood. You won't find it on any map because no one is supposed to know it exists. That will be where he is, I'm sure of it."

"What about the assassin he has guarding him?" Dante asked.

"What assassin?" Diabhal responded.

"He said it was the Merchant of Death or something, from the Hallowed Shroud," Dante responded.

"The Merchant of Death?" Diabhal questioned. "You said he was working with young Damon?"

"Yes, somebody who was making copies of himself," Dante answered.

"You don't need to explain, I know who you're talking about. The man you're describing is the only person in the world more dangerous than young Damon and me combined. I can't understand why he would be working for young Damon, though. Perhaps he needed him for whatever meeting he was headed toward," Diabhal pondered aloud. "If we're lucky, he won't be there. If we're unlucky, we won't leave. But the assassins from the Hallowed Shroud are not ones to act as bodyguards, even for a hefty sum of gold."

"How do you know so much about them? Old friends of yours?" Aliyah asked.

"No, just the opposite," Diabhal answered. "I have killed three of their blades before. People hired them to kill my King, and I stopped them. Luckily, they never sent their best. This doesn't change my plan. We will still march on Stormhelm and hope whatever work the Merchant of Death was doing for young Damon is over."

"So we just walk in and kill Damon?" Dante asked.

"No," Diabhal answered. "If we try to charge the gate, we will likely die. The castle is armed with multiple traps. Even if we were to make it through, it would be unlikely that young Damon would still be there. He will escape in the chaos, and our window will be gone."

"What should we do then?" Aliyah asked.

"We will enter the castle under the cover of night and sneak past any guards there are. I doubt Stormhelm is the same as I remember her, but I also doubt much has changed, so we will take caution as we travel through," Diabhal explained.

"And if we accidentally alert the guards?" Dante questioned.

"Then we fail," Daibhal stated. "You will surely die, and young Damon will be nearly impossible to find after that."

"Well, let's try to avoid that then," Dante said with a nervous laugh.

"You should rest now so we can start our journey at sunset. We need to move under the cover of darkness," Diabhal suggested.

"That makes sense," Aliyah sighed. "Besides, I'm desperately sleepy anyway."

"Me too," Dante agreed as he relaxed back onto his mat.

Diabhal said nothing else. Instead, he stared at the campfire while everyone else drifted off to sleep. He caught some rest while everyone else was digging graves, so he felt fine and ready to take watch for the last few hours of the day.

As soon as Dante closed his eyes, he could feel himself drifting off to sleep. The last couple of days had taken a toll on his body, and he was exhausted. Within minutes, he slipped into a dream state, lost in his own thoughts.

Suddenly, the blackness of sleep began to change. Shades of green and blue began to pop into light, slowly coming into clarity until Dante found himself back underneath the maple tree on the hill. He recognized it from the last dream he had, but he still had no clue where he was. However, all of his questions vanished once he saw Faetu sitting on the edge of the hilltop.

"Ah, Dante, there you are," Faetu said, slapping his hand on the ground next to him. "Come have a seat."

"Faetu?!" Dante exclaimed. "Is that really you?"

"Of course it is, who else would I be?" Faetu replied.

Dante nearly burst into tears as he ran over to his friend and hugged him. He was on the edge of sobbing into Faetu's shoulder as he tried his best to contain his emotions.

"I'm so sorry, Faetu. I'm sorry I was too weak to help you," Dante said as a tear fell down his cheek.

"You don't need to apologize," Faetu responded. "I was destined to fail so you could succeed."

Dante let Faetu go and looked at him, confused. He sat down next to him and asked, "What do you mean by that?"

"I mean, it is your turn in the spotlight, Dante. You have greatness within you that has yet to show, I just know it."

"But what do you mean by that? What greatness?"

"It's not my place to tell you, but you will see soon enough," Faetu said with a wink.

"I don't get it," Dante said in confusion.

"And you don't have to," Faetu responded. "So, what have you done since our battle with Damon?"

"We were taken prisoner and hauled off to Angron Prison," Dante answered. "But, we accidentally ran into someone there who was willing to help us. Apparently, he knows Damon from long ago, and his power is a weakness to Damon."

"What's his power?" Faetu asked.

"He controls fire, kind of like yours, except his is black," Dante answered.

"A black flame," Faetu pondered aloud, "That is interesting."

"We broke him out of prison," Dante continued. "Well, we broke him out of his chains, and he did most of the rest. He fights like a devil, it's actually kind of frightening."

"Do you trust him?" Faetu asked.

"No," Dante answered sharply. "I think he would kill us if he felt like it, but he seems honest when he says he wants the head of the King. However, I can tell he is a monster on the inside. Something about him is off-putting and makes me uneasy; I just can't pin it down.
We are going to infiltrate a castle he knows about and, hopefully, kill Damon there, ending his reign of terror forever and getting vengeance for you and Aslan. Damon's last days draw near."

"And this man you freed, once Damon is what about him?" Faetu asked.

"He says he is adamant about putting all of this to rest after he's done with Damon, so hopefully he just walks off into the sunset, never to be heard from again," Dante guessed.

"And what if he doesn't?" Faetu questioned.

"Then I guess I'll try to cross that bridge when I get to it and hope the bridge doesn't burn me alive," Dante answered as he stared off into the distance, "But if he tried to kill me, there'd be nothing I could do about it. He's too strong."

"You're stronger than you give yourself credit for," Faetu complimented.

"You haven't seen what this guy can do. He moves like Damon did, but scarier," Dante dismissed.

"I still say not to count yourself out," Faetu said as he patted Dante on the back for encouragement.

Dante sat in silence for a moment before saying, "What should I do?"

"What do you mean?" Faetu asked.

"Guide me," Dante stated. "Tell me what I need to do next. It's just me, Aliyah, and Kinomaru. They need you... I need you. I can't do this without your help."

"You can, and you will. Just trust your instincts. The rest will fall into place as it should, I'm sure of it. How is Aliyah doing?"

"She's grieving, we all are, but she misses you especially."

"You know, it was never my place to be by her side anyway. You need to be there to comfort her," Faetu instructed.

Dante started to stumble over his words as his cheeks flushed, saying, "W-what do you mean?"

"I see the way you look at her, Dante," Faetu said with a laugh. "I know how you've felt about her all our lives. It's no secret, at least not to me. You should tell her how you feel."

Dante sighed before saying, "I can't. It's not the time."

"It's never the time, but you should say it anyway. You'll feel better if you finally get it off your chest. Besides, even if she rejects you, she'll let you down easy."

"Maybe, but we have bigger things to worry about right now," Dante dismissed.

"If you say so," Faetu said with a shrug.

"Now, please, tell me what to do about Damon."

"As I already said, you have to do that on your own."

"But why, Faetu? Why can't you help me?" Dante said, growing frustrated with his friend's refusal to help.

"Because this is your path to walk. My lead led us to failure and to my death. You don't need my guidance, you need to trust your own," Faetu said calmly.

"But I can't do this," Dante said as he rested his head on his knees. "I'm too weak. How can I succeed where you failed?"

"Because you're better than me," Faetu stated.

Dante started to chuckle as he said, "I never took you for a jester."

"I'm telling no lies, you are destined to do great things, Dante. You will go on to accomplish so much more than I ever could," Faetu assured.

"I still don't see why you say these things, Faetu," Dante said as he raised his head.

As soon as Dante looked back at Faetu, he scrambled backward in terror. Faetu's body sat next to him, headless. Blood began to soak the clothing around his neck, and he held his severed head in his lap.

"What's the matter, Dante?" Faetu asked, speaking from the severed head. "Is something the matter?"

Dante began to breathe heavily as the horrifying imagery of his friend in this state was anxiety-inducing. He scrambled to find the words to speak, but nothing would come out of his lips. He was dumbfounded and didn't know what to say.

"Dante?" Faetu asked. "Dan… te?"

His voice trailed off into a strange tone as the world around him started to fall apart. Dante was in a panic as he fearfully tried to cling to any footing he could, but everything began to crumble to pieces. In a crazed panic, Dante felt like he was drifting into madness. His lungs stopped working, and he couldn't take a breath, no matter how hard he tried. It was as if his body refused to listen.

Finally, he took in a gasp of breath as he sat up in a panic. He looked around to see that he was back at the campsite, and the sun was starting to set. Kinomaru and Aliyah were still asleep, but Diabhal was sitting by the fire in the same place he was when he laid down.

"Bad dream?" Diabhal asked.

"Yes," Dante answered. "Tell me something. How do you deal with the death of close ones so easily? How come it doesn't bother you?"

"It did," Diabhal answered. "It used to tear me apart, haunt my dreams, and tear at my mind. But when you live in torment for long enough, it starts to feel comfortable. Eventually, you grow numb to the loss, and it becomes second nature to you."

Dante sighed as he shook his head. He didn't want to feel the grief anymore, but he didn't want to become numb to the loss either. He found himself at an uncomfortable crossroads, and he felt incapable of deciding either way.

"We should leave soon. We don't want to lose any darkness while we can use it," Diabhal said as he stood to his feet. "Wake your friends."

Dante acknowledged him with a quick nod and looked at the fire for a moment before standing to his feet. He walked over and gave Kinomaru a nudge on the arm to wake him up and then knelt to gently shake Aliyah's shoulder and wake her as well.

"Is it time already?" Aliyah asked as she rubbed her eyes.

"Unfortunately, yes,' Dante said with a chuckle. "We should get moving while we have cover."

Dante tried to stand when Aliyah grabbed him by the wrist and said, "Hey."

Dante looked down at his wrist, then at Aliyah, and his cheeks started to flush, "Y-yes?"

"Thank you," Aliyah said softly.

"F-for what?" Dante stuttered.

"For being there and helping me see reason when I had all but given up. We've been going nonstop since we left the wagon, so I hadn't had the chance to say it. I really appreciate that, Dante. I am grateful to you," Aliyah said with a slight smile as she loosened her grip on Dante's wrist.

Dante's heart beat out of his chest. He had waited years for a chance to tell Aliyah how he felt, and for the first time in his life, the moment felt right.

"Now's the time," Dante thought to himself. "Just tell her how you feel, and if you burn up in the process, so be it."

He cleared his throat and said, "I promise that I wasn't doing it because I had to, I care about you. Listen, Aliyah, there's something I want to tell you."

"What is it?" Aliyah asked curiously.

Dante took a breath as he scrambled to put the thoughts together, "I don't really know how to word this, but I-"

"Hey," Diabhal shouted from the edge of the camp. "If you're coming, let's go."

They snapped their attention over toward Diabhal, and then Dante let out a sigh of defeat as he said, "He's right, we should go."

"What was it you wanted to tell me?" Aliyah prodded.

"It's nothing important, I'll tell you later," Dante said with a fake smile.

"Okay," Aliyah said as she stood, "but don't forget it, I want to hear your thoughts, deal?"

"Deal," Dante agreed.

Aliyah started walking away, and Dante watched her step through the camp. He let out a long sigh, and his head hung slightly. He felt Kinomaru place his hand on his shoulder, and he turned to see his friend smiling at him like he always does. Kinomaru nodded his head slightly, and Dante returned the smile in kind.

"I know," Dante muttered, "I'll tell her eventually."

Kinomaru patted Dante on the shoulder and then walked onward to join the others. Dante followed behind him, and the four of them began their trip south. The sun was just beginning to disappear behind the horizon, so they had plenty of night hours left to travel.

The trip would take them two more days to reach their destination. Along the way, they stayed incredibly quiet. The farther south they traveled, the more of Damon's men they saw, and they didn't want anyone to catch on to their approach. They would hide behind cover for hours at a time as they waited for the right moment to move, leading to an incredibly slow but safe approach to the castle.

While they waited, they didn't speak. They would use Diabhal's dark flames to heat any food they needed to, and made sure to keep themselves as invisible as they could. During the night, they walked more often and made sure to stay near cover when they needed to duck quickly.

Halfway into the third night of their journey, they found themselves hiding behind cover as they waited for a patrol to walk far enough away for them to move. They were drawing incredibly close to the castle, and had already seen it from far away earlier in the daylight hours, but they still had a short distance to cover before they could sneak in.

As they sat in waiting, Dante looked around at their surroundings. He had never been this far south before, so the landscape was completely alien to him. It wasn't easy to see, but the moonlight provided just enough light for him to take in the basic topography. At first, he looked in quiet admiration, but then something confused him.

In the distance to the east, he saw a particularly familiar mountain. He didn't know why, but he was sure he had seen it before. Something about it was familiar to him, but he couldn't pinpoint what it was. He became lost in thought as he stared at the mountain until a tap on his chest snapped his attention back to the group.

Aliyah waved for him to move as the rest of the group had already started to walk, so Dante quickly followed. He glanced back over at the mountain one more time, but still couldn't decipher why he recognized it, so he ignored it and kept moving.

Under the cover of darkness, they shuffled across the last grassy field between them and Castle Stormhelm.

Chapter 10

They made their final approach to the castle and were in awe that such a fortress wasn't on a map of any kind. The castle walls stretched up into the air, but were covered in moss and not well-maintained. There were battered siege weapons that adorned the tops of towers, and some of the merlons had been crumbled or knocked from the walls and sat in heaps of rubble just outside.

Despite the castle's aged condition, it was still very much lived in. Light emanated from within the walls, illuminating from the inside and giving the castle an even more ominous appearance against the dark night sky behind it. There were guards that could periodically be seen patrolling the ramparts, but most of the movement within could only be spotted by the traveling shadows that flowed with the moving torchlight.

They pressed themselves against the cold stone wall as they followed Diabhal along the perimeter. He seemed to know where he was going, so they followed his lead and hoped they wouldn't get caught. After walking nearly halfway around the castle, they stopped midway along the southern wall.

Dante looked curiously as he watched Diabhal stare at the wall as if he were studying the masonry. Eventually, his eyes snapped to a particular stone, and he shifted a few feet away and dropped down to the ground.

"What is he doing?" Dante thought to himself.

Diabhal started digging into the grass with his bare hands, pulling up small clumps of dirt a little at a time. After he removed about six inches of soil, he reached into the ground and planted his feet as if he were pulling on something. The ground began to lift in a perfect rectangle around him, and they realized he was pulling on a covered cellar door. Kinomaru bent down and grabbed the door from underneath, helping Diabhal pull the door completely open, revealing a dusty set of stairs that descended underneath the castle.

Diabhal gave them a nod toward the stairs, telling them to go, and they filed down the stairs one at a time. Diabhal waited until they were all inside before he followed after, pulling the door closed behind him and trying his best to leave as few traces as possible.

Once they were inside, Diabhal moved his way back to the front of the group and placed a finger over his mouth. They followed him down the dark stairs slowly, but the silence in the room was deafening. The lack of light gave them reason to believe no one was ahead of them, but it also made it hard for them to see where they were going, so they moved as slowly as possible.

They felt like they had traveled down a hundred stairs when Diabhal suddenly stopped them. Worry spiked and sent a rush down their spine, but then they heard him grab a torch from the wall and light it. His black flame didn't burn as brightly as a normal one, but it was more than enough light for them to see what was around them.

As the light stretched to every corner of their room, they saw that they were in an abandoned study. There were shelves of decaying books lining the walls, plush furniture that was falling apart, and a round table in the center of the room that looked like it once held important meetings. However, crumpled at the edges of the table were the remains of two people, decayed to bones, and left to rot.

"This is my King," Diabhal spoke suddenly, startling the rest of the group. "My King and my general."

"You mean they are who Damon killed all those years ago?" Dante asked.

"Yes, right where we stand. This is where the tide of power shifted in young Damon's favor, and he went from the son of a general to the King of an empire. This is where my freedom came to an end, and the monster I created was finally brought to light," Diabhal explained.

"Are you saying they were just left here after they were killed?" Aliyah asked.

"So it would seem. Young Damon stood right here where I am and raised his hand to my King. I could have stopped him, and I should have stopped him, but I hesitated. The nightmare inside of me, who had no problem laying waste to thousands of innocent lives, hesitated. Because of my failures, my King and my general were both killed right in front of me," Diabhal stated, expressing an emotion that the rest of the group thought he was incapable of feeling.

"Why do you think he left them here?" Dante asked.

"I don't know. Despite what he did, he loved his father. Even after watching him do it, I never thought he would have taken the life of his old man. Maybe he left these two here because he didn't want to face what he had done. Or, maybe he left them here because he felt they weren't worth the effort it took to bury them. Only young Damon knows."

"Do you want to pay your respects?" Aliyah asked.

"What would that accomplish? It will not bring them back. It will not wipe my mistake from history. It won't restore young Damon to the man he should have been. No. I have no respects to pay, nor rituals to perform. The only thing left for me to do is behead the viper that coils around my mind. Once he is dead, I will be free to put this to rest for good," Diabhal stated. "You see, the corpses of Kings and nobles are but a testament that the weapons that ended their lives are above all of us, for the edge of a blade can cut down royalty and peasants the same. No, the only thing I need to pay respect to is the blade that will make another King's corpse before sunrise."

They listened to his words and felt a cold chill run down their spines. The malice in his intent was visible as his hand clenched around the torch he was holding. They could feel the hatred radiating from him like a wave of oppressive energy, and it was unsettling. They paused where they were as they waited to see where to go next, but Diabhal just stared at the corpse of his King.

After a few moments, he turned away from the skeletons and started walking toward the back corner of the room. Everyone else began to follow, but were startled when he suddenly stopped in his tracks.

"Damnit," Diabhal muttered.

"What is it?" Dante asked.

"We can't go this way," Diabhal answered as he held his torch up and illuminated a crumbled and caved-in hallway. Rubble filled the walkway from top to bottom, leaving no room to slip through, even for a small animal. "This tunnel led to the main chambers of the castle. We'll have to find another way inside."

"What about this way?" Aliyah asked.

Diabhal walked over to her and saw she was pointing at a hole in the wall. The hole was just big enough for a person to crouch through, but Kinomaru would have to crawl. However, on the other side of the hole, it appeared to be a tunnel of some kind.

"It's our only option, unless we want to go back out the way we came," Diabhal explained.

"We'll follow your lead," Dante stated.

"Stay behind me and stay quiet," Diabhal ordered.

He tossed the torch through the hole and slipped through, surveying the area as he waited for everyone else to follow. Once the last person came through, he led them down the tunnel. They weren't sure where they were, but Diabhal seemed to know where he was going, so they trusted his judgement.

It didn't take long before Diabhal choked out the flame of the torch, set it aside, and started to move more quietly. The tunnel seemed to slope upward, with multiple smaller-looking drains that appeared to connect to it at various points. Dante assumed it was a drainage system of some kind, but wasn't certain.

As they continued to climb the tunnel, they began to hear voices from the connecting pipes, signaling that they were close to the surface, and the moonlight at the tunnel's end served as a lighthouse guiding them to their destination.

They slowly approached the end of the tunnel and saw it stopped at a metal grate fastened into the stonework of the castle. It was within the castle walls, but outside of the main chambers. Diabhal slowly poked his head out of the grate and looked around to see that there were no guards posted nearby, but the hole wasn't big enough for them to fit through, so they had to come up with a way to get out.

Diabhal didn't say anything to anyone before he grabbed a hold of one of the bars and started to melt the metal under his grip, just as he did to the gate of the prison. He slowly worked his way around the circumference of the grate, melting the bars one at a time. The action wasn't silent, but it wasn't too loud either, so they waited until he was down to the final two bars that held the grate in place.

He placed his hand on one of the bars to start to melt it, but the grate suddenly slipped from its position within the stone and quickly fell downward at an angle. Diabhal was caught off guard by the sudden slipping and was ill-prepared to catch the grate. He threw his arms up to grab the grate, hoping to muffle the sound, but it nearly knocked him to the ground.

However, before it smashed into the stone below, Kinomaru caught the grate and stopped it mere inches from the ground. The grate was heavy, but once he established control of it, he was able to place it beside them gently. The only noise that rang out was the sound of the small rocks that hit the ground when the bars broke free.

Diabhal quickly popped his head back out of the hole and looked around, waiting patiently to see if anyone heard the rocks, but there didn't seem to be any movement around them. Once a few seconds of silence had passed, Diabhal climbed out of the hole and quickly made his way over to a building for cover.

One by one, the others climbed out as well and followed Diabhal's lead. The hole was in the center of a more open area, but the buildings were close enough that no one on the walls would have spotted the hole or them crawling out of it. Once they were all out of the tunnel and ready to continue, Diabhal waved them on, and they slowly started to walk between the buildings.

They crept onward, slower than they had moved at any point before, but closer to being caught than they cared to risk. The sounds of guards speaking were clear enough to listen to, as some of them were no more than a few feet away on the opposite side of the walls. Getting caught likely meant certain death for some of them, and they were all too aware of how hopelessly outnumbered they were.

Diabhal led them closer to the main chambers, but they had a significant distance to cover without being spotted by the dozens of men between them and their destination. They slipped from one alleyway to the next until they could see the final building between them and the main chambers. The building was large and acted as a barrier between the courtyard and the bridge to the keep.

Once they reached the edge of the alleyway they were in, there was an open area they had to cross before reaching the last obstacle. Inside the open area, a pathway led to a ledge that dropped down a level to match the rest of the courtyard. The drop was only a few feet, but it didn't have any railing that would stop them from jumping down. Diabhal looked around for a while, surveying any potential lines of sight.

Once he assessed it was clear to move, he quickly and quietly darted for the ledge. Dante was quick to follow, with Aliyah after him and Kinomaru bringing up the rear. They slipped over the edge one by one until Kinomaru jumped down with them. However, as soon as they were all over the ledge, their hearts sank.

"What was that?" a voice rang out from the direction they came from.

They all quickly pressed themselves against the wall beneath the ledge, trying their best to avoid being seen, but they could hear footsteps slowly approaching. Each step felt like an explosion in their ears as it meant they were one step closer to being caught. They didn't know what to do, and there was nowhere for them to go. One foot after another crunched the rocks and gravel as they carried a man closer and closer to their location.

"Damnit, we're too close to get caught now," Dante thought to himself. "What do we do?"

The man casually strolled closer to the edge, and they could tell he was only a few feet away, which meant he was two steps away from finding them and their lives getting significantly worse. Dante placed his hand on his sword, ready to strike as soon as he saw his chance, but another voice interrupted the incredibly tense silence.

"Hey, you almost done out here?" a different voice yelled out.

"Hang on a sec, I thought I saw somethin' over here," the closer man yelled back.

"We don't got time to hang on, you're up on the dice," the second man yelled back, clearly intoxicated.

They heard the closer man sigh and said, "Alright, I'm comin'."

The footsteps grew quieter as they moved farther away, and eventually, they heard a door close. They breathed a collective sigh of relief as they waited to make sure no one would be watching. Once they checked to be sure, they scrambled across the small open area and reached the final building. However, as soon as they reached the building, they all rapidly scrambled to the side to tuck themselves away.

Just inside the window, they spotted dozens of guards all lounging around, with plenty more sleeping in bunks off to the side. The building had been converted to a barracks and was filled to the brim with people. This posed a significant problem because there was no way to bypass the guardhouse. The only way to reach the keep and get into the main chamber was to go through.

Daibhal pointed to a vining plant that climbed up the side of the building and ended at the roof. The plant seemed years old, with its tendrils deeply anchored in all manner of cracks and crevices. It looked sturdy enough to support all of their weight, even Kinomaru's.

Near the top of the vine was an open window that looked to be on the second floor of the building. Dante had no clue what was up there, but Diabhal seemed intent on leading them through it, and he saw no other path. He nodded to their guide, and Diabhal started climbing the vine and scaling the wall to the second floor.

Dante nodded for Aliyah to go before him, and then motioned Kinomaru to follow her. One by one, the group climbed the vine and slipped into the window as quietly as possible. Once Kinomaru entered the window, Dante began to climb as well, slowly reaching hand over hand, scaling the wall as fast as he could. He was nervous being in the open, so he never looked back. He reached into the window and grabbed the frame to pull himself through and get out of sight.

As soon as his feet touched the ground, he was stunned to see someone just across the room, lying in bed. He quickly glanced in every direction to see where everyone had gone, and spotted them near the doorway to the room, behind a pillar. He quickly scurried over to join them, and Diabhal waved them onward to continue moving.

The second floor of the guardhouse was centered around an atrium of sorts. The center of the building was open to the ceiling, and the second floor wrapped around the opening, secured with a railing. They could hear the guards talking below, and, luckily for them, the noise helped mask their movements.

They stayed as far away from the railing as possible as they carefully navigated from pillar to pillar until they reached the other side of the building. They checked the first room they found to see if the window would get them where they needed to go, but Diabhal quickly jerked his head backward the moment he saw a guard sitting on his bed reading a book. He shook his head no and moved to the next room. He slowly peeked his head inside and saw that the room was empty, so he ushered the rest of the group in.

Dante immediately went to the window and slowly opened it, revealing the bridge to the keep on the other side. He looked down and tried to find something to hang onto, but there were no vines on the side of the building. As he continued to look for a way across, Kinomaru nudged him on the arm to step aside.

Dante moved aside and let his friend have a peek, but was surprised to see him immediately start climbing out of the window. Kinomaru grabbed the windowsill and slowly began to lower himself down until only the tip of his fingers was supporting his weight. Once he was that low, his feet were not too far from the ground, and dropping down was of no consequence.

Kinomaru landed with a thud, but thankfully, it wasn't loud enough to draw any attention. Once he landed, he raised his arms back up toward the window and motioned for the rest of them to jump. Aliyah was the first to jump, landing easily in Kinomaru's arms. Dante followed directly after, landing safely just as Aliyah did.

Diabhal was hesitant to jump toward Kinomaru. He took some extra time to check his surroundings and see if there was another safe way down, but didn't find any. With no other options, Diabhal jumped down toward Kinomaru, who caught him and quickly placed him down on the ground.

Diabhal gave him a nod of thanks, and the four of them promptly moved across the bridge and toward the doors of the keep.

"I can't believe we've made it this far without something going wrong," Dante thought to himself. "We're one doorway away from putting an end to this and getting revenge for our friends. Damon will breathe his last today."

The bridge took only a minute to cross, and, luckily for everyone, it was devoid of guards. The path between them and the keep door was clear, and all they had to do was run. Step after step, they moved as quickly across as they could.

Once they crossed, they saw a singular door sat at the end of the bridge, and nothing more. They stopped for a second to slow their breathing and prepare themselves for the battle that waited for them on the other side. Once everyone was ready, Dante reached for the handle and jumped as soon as his hand touched the door.

A thunderous horn rang out from above the keep that rattled their chests and echoed off the walls of the castle. The sound was disorienting and terrifyingly loud. Everyone immediately knew they had been caught.

“Damnit, in minutes the entire castle will be bearing down on us,” Diabhal growled.

“What do we do?” Aliyah asked.

“Go ahead and get to young Damon. Kill him while I deal with everyone else. If you can’t kill him, stall him long enough for me to,” Diabhal instructed.

"But only you can get through his barrier. We'll get shredded if we try," Danted argued.

"You don't have a choice. I would suggest you all stay back and hold them off while I go in, but you'll be slaughtered, and I'll have to deal with everyone. I can't fight young Damon and all his men at the same time," Diabhal growled.

"No," an unfamiliar voice spoke, startling them. "You go, I'll stay behind."

Dante and Aliyah looked at Kinomaru with wide eyes. They couldn't believe what they were hearing. He had never muttered a single sound since they met him, and now he is speaking as if he could all along.

Kinomaru took a deep breath and let it out slowly; he looked almost afraid. He grabbed his hammer off his back and gently placed it upside down on the ground in front of him with the handle pointing up.

"Kinomaru…" Dante said, astounded.

"They need your help to kill Damon, so you will go," Kinomaru demanded.

"You're strong, but you aren't strong enough to take on the entire army," Diabhal stated.

"At my full strength, I could crush you between my fingers, Diabhal. You were right about me being Idrasi," Kinomaru said coldly.

"I see," Diabhal digressed, giving truth to his words.

"Kinomaru, I have so many questions," Dante said. "Why have you never spoken to us before?"

"I will speak quickly, as I don't have much time left. My people draw power from the magic in the universe around us. We have been blessed with the Idrasi Incantations, a set of incredibly powerful and ancient magics that turn our bodies into weapons of destruction. My people have used these incantations to protect our homeland countless times, but we wanted nothing but peace.

Many tried to take our lands and steal our incantations for their own foul use, but all of them failed. None tried more than the warlord Razghul. He could not live with his numerous failures, so he gave his life and that of his dynasty to curse the Idrasi people into extinction. Our most powerful weapon was turned against us, and any of us who muttered a word were damned to die soon after. We lost nearly everyone before we figured out what had happened. The only reason I lived was because my mother woke me and insisted I stay silent. I may very well be the last of the Idrasi left," Kinomaru explained.

"Wait, does that mean?" Aliyah suddenly said, her lip beginning to quiver.

"Yes, now I will die," Kinomaru answered. "But my death is worth it to help you. You took me in when I had nowhere to go, and accepted me without hesitation. You are more family than I ever had, and I have cherished these years. I am especially grateful to you, Dante. You have always treated me like you treat everyone else, even if our conversations were one-sided."

A tear fell from Dante's eye as he said, "No, Kinomaru, please tell me there is something I can do. I don't want to lose anyone else."

"My fate was sealed the moment I spoke," Kinomaru said with his trademark smile. "Now, go. As long as I breathe, no one will slip past me."

"I don't know what to say," Dante muttered as he experienced a whirlwind of emotion.

"Don't say anything," Kinomaru insisted. "Just go and kill Damon. Avenge Faetu and Aslan, and end his tyranny. Save the Devalon Empire from the rule of a violent tyrant. I have already lived longer than everyone I grew up with. It's finally time to rejoin them. Oh, and my real name is Kyojin, but Kinomaru is still fine."

"Come on, we have to go before young Damon escapes," Daibhal insisted.

"Thank you, Kinomaru," Aliyah said before she followed Diabhal through the door.

Dante stood frozen for a moment as he looked at the warming smile on Kinomaru's face. He couldn't believe everything he was hearing, and he had the same feeling he had at the graves of Faetu and Aslan. He didn't want to walk away.

"It's okay, Dante, I'm content with my decision. Besides, it's too late to go back now. I was given a second chance at life when I met all of you. This is my way of paying you back," Kinomaru assured.

Dante could see he meant what he said, but that didn't make the idea of losing another close friend any easier. He spoke with a shaky voice, "Thank you, Kinomaru. Thank you for everything. I had no idea you lived with such a weight hanging over your shoulders. If I had known, I would have tried to help."

"You helped more than you know," Kinomaru stated. "You are a kind man, and a cherished friend. I will tell stories about you to my people in the afterlife. Goodbye, Dante."

Dante slowly took a step back as he watched Kinomaru turn to face the opposite side of the bridge. Then he picked up his pace and hurried through the door, closing it behind him and locking the bolt.

Kinomaru knelt behind his hammer and placed his hands on his knees. He took in a deep breath as he started to hear footsteps trampling on the opposite side of the bridge. He closed his eyes and began to mutter one of the ancient incantations of his people.

"Sai gabe lombulombu ma dagingku, palungku gabe hujur na mangalo hajahaton, jala matangku gabe lensa na so boi buni sipaotooto," As Kinomaru spoke, his body began to change. Bands of white-hot energy began to wrap around his limbs like ribbons. "Di toru ni borat ni palungku, dapotan paradianan parpudi do angka na mangalului hamagoan," he continued as his eyes started to glow white and energy began to radiate outward from his body as if he were teeming with power. "Sai dipalu ma hasapi ni Dagda sada ende na mambahen mudarhu gabe bahan bakar na manutung api ni tondingku jala pagalakhon rimas ni bangsongku. Di ari on, huperjuangkan do asi ni roha ni Dagda," he said as he completed his incantation.

He placed his hand on the handle of his hammer, and the ribbons of energy on his arm immediately wrapped around the shaft until they collected at the head of the weapon, giving it a menacingly powerful appearance. He stood to his feet and looked across the bridge at the hundreds of men charging at him.

"Mother... Father... I will be home soon," he softly spoke to himself. "I hope I've made you proud."

Chapter 11

Dante placed his hand on the door as he heard the death throes of the first few men to meet Kinomaru's wrath. He turned to see Diabhal had already started advancing up the stairs and toward a large door at the top. He and Aliyah quickly followed behind and chased him.

As they topped the stairwell, they saw Diabhal had already opened the door, and their hearts beat out of their chest. Standing at the other side of the room was none other than King Damon, the man they were here to kill.

"Diabhal, old friend, I had heard you escaped from the prison, but I didn't think you would make it here so fast," Damon declared. "Nevertheless, you have simply saved me the time it would have taken to hunt you down and gut you myself. I told you I couldn't allow a monster like you to walk freely, knowing you oppose my rule."

"It's time, young Damon," Diabhal muttered.

"I told you I would let you live because of our history, which is a grace I have given no one before or after you," Damon muttered. "But you spit in my face and ally yourself with those who recently tried to kill me. It's clear what your intentions are, Diabhal."

"I am here to do what I should have done all those years ago," Diabhal said.

"I'll admit, I'm impressed you made it as far as you have," Damon said as he stared at the three people across from him. "But this place will soon be swarming with my men."

"You'll find that unlikely to happen," Diabhal stated. "Now, it's time."

"I decide what time it is, Diabhal. If I wished for it to be midnight at noon, you would find the sun retreating in fear. I knew I should have killed you all those years ago," Damon grunted.

"But you didn't. Instead, you left me to rot and suffer in solitude. Now grab your sword and face your death with honor," Diabhal said as the black flames crawled around the edge of his blade as they had before.

"You would dare raise your hand to your King?" Damon asked arrogantly.

"You are no King. People like us are dogs of war. We are not fit to lead anything other than armies into battle. Our skills are only useful in taking the lives of those who oppose us. They are useless when seated on a throne. It's time to go, young Damon," Diabhal spoke in a surprisingly calm and comforting tone, as if he felt sorrow for what he was about to do.

Damon looked past Diabhal at Dante and said, "I must give you credit, you have taught me something this day. Once I've dealt with all of you, I will make sure I never leave anyone alive again. I will travel to Dawnberry and raze it to the ground. Every poor soul walking those streets will greet you in hell once I'm through."

Dante's eyes widened as Damon spoke, causing him to laugh in amusement before saying, "Oh, you thought I had forgotten you? Did you think I had forgotten the poor, weak boy whose face met the soil beneath my heel? No, I remember everything. I will take the life of everyone in your pathetic village, just as I did your caretaker."

"You're going to die, Damon," Dante shouted as his trembling hands placed a firm grip on his sword. "For everything you've put us through."

"I've heard that before," Damon said as he rolled his eyes. "You will join all those who failed before you, including your pathetic friends."

"Enough speech, young Damon. Draw your blade," Diabhal demanded.

King Damon grabbed his sword with a grin, but Dante could see something was different about him. When they faced him in the forest, he seemed completely unbothered. But when faced against Diabhal, he seemed nervous. The tension in the room was thick, and Dante waited patiently for one of them to make the first move.

"This is for Faetu," Aliyah mumbled under her breath.

She quickly drew back her bow and loosed an arrow that flew directly toward Damon, but the arrow shattered just an inch away from his eye. However, the arrow was all it took to send the room into a frenzy.

Damon quickly went on the offensive and rocketed toward Diabhal with inhuman speed. The two slammed into one another and attacked at a pace that Dante's eyes could barely keep up with. Black flames and sparks spurted out in multiple directions as the two clashed swords, creating a whirlwind of devastating power in the center of the room.

"Is this what real power looks like?" Dante thought to himself as he watched the two go at it. "We don't stand a chance against someone like this."

Diabhal swung his blade at Damon's head, but the attack was parried. Damon retaliated by throwing a quick jab that dotted Diabhal on the nose, but he was also kicked in the leg and knocked off balance. Diabhal tried to swoop around and swing his sword upward at Damon's neck before he could regain his footing, but Damon blocked the attack and slammed Diabhal in the chest with a powerful gust of wind that sent him sliding backward.

"I have to try and do something," Dante thought as he took a step forward and looked for an opening to strike.

Aliyah loosed arrow after arrow, hoping that one of them would get through, but each one seemed to slam into the barrier that Diabhal mentioned. However, she refused to stand idly by and continued to attack.

Diabhal swayed backward to avoid a swing of Damon's sword, lifted his leg to avoid a kick, ducked underneath a wild backfist, and parried Damon's sword on his follow-up strike. Each attack that Damon threw was either dodged, blocked, or parried, and the only time he was able to land any offense was weak punches that were thrown quickly instead of with power.

"Face it, young Damon," Diabhal said with sadness in his voice as he dodged attacks. "You cannot best me in battle."

"You will find that I've grown much stronger than you remember," Damon declared as he took a deep breath. He let it out slowly and said, "You will die today."

"I already planned on it," Diabhal grunted as he dashed in for a strike.

Damon took a quick step back to avoid the strike and tried to counter, but Diabhal had already regained his center of gravity and dodged his attack as well. Damon was forced to duck under the black flame-covered sword, but was met with a powerful knee that slammed into his face.

Dante saw this as his chance to strike. He was terrified of getting close and could feel adrenaline coursing through his body. He jumped in and slammed his blade downward at Damon's face, hoping to sneak an attack in after he was recently struck, but the sword stopped just before it hit.

Damon watched the blade come directly to the center of his eyes, but knew it wouldn't land. However, he was stunned to see the edge of the sword start to twitch and nudge itself closer for a moment before the weapon was pulled back. Damon wasn't sure how he was doing it, but he had already seen enough of the sidekicks Diabhal had brought with him.

Dante pulled his sword back but was stunned to feel his body move almost on impulse. He leaned to the side to avoid an attack that would have sliced him in two. Damon's blade passed so close to his body that it sheared some of the fabric from his shirt. Dante was stunned at what had just happened, but didn't have time to process it as he saw another attack coming.

"You're fight is with me," Diabhal shouted as he swung his blade hard at Damon's neck.

Dante watched Damon closely, hoping to dodge the next attack that he threw, but was shocked when he felt the burning sting of a sword slicing through his arm. Out of the corner of his eye, he saw Diabhal's blade cut a gash into his upper arm before Damon deflected it. He jumped to the side and grabbed his arm in pain as he realized that Diabhal would just as easily kill him as he would Damon.

"I'm going to have to keep myself away from both of their attacks if I want to see the end of this," Dante thought to himself. He winced as he felt the warmth of his blood soaking into the sleeve of his tunic, thinking, "Damnit, this hurts like hells."

Dante rushed back in, trying his best to assist Diabhal in killing Damon. He saw Damon parry an attack and tried to step in, but the King was too fast. Damon swayed back to avoid Diabhal's blade, kicked Dante's sword to the side, and threw a quick thrusting attack at Diabhal. He watched his old mentor avoid the attack and tried to follow up with a thunderously powerful strike.

Damon channeled his energy into his palm, just as he did when he struck Kinomaru, and thrusted it toward Diabhal at incredible speed. However, he was stunned to see Dante slam his blade upward into the bottom of his arm. The attack wasn't enough to break through his barrier, but the force was enough to deflect the strike and save Diabhal.

Dante grinned as he finally felt like he had done something useful, but saw Damon also had a smirk on his face. The power that was collected in the King's palm streamed across his chest and gathered in the opposite hand. Dante saw Damon let go of his sword, draw back his opposite hand, and thrust it toward him in less than a second, but was unable to recover from the force he threw into parrying the initial attack.

Damon's hand slammed into Dante's abdomen, and a wave of force erupted from the point of impact. A stream of gray-tinted energy blasted out of Dante's back, and he felt like a raging bull had just ripped entirely through his body. He gasped for air, but his body wouldn't listen. The attack lifted him off the ground, and he was sure he was dead.

Before his sword hit the ground, Damon drew his arm back and tried to catch his blade, but was furious to hear an arrow strike the weapon and knock it out of his reach. Diabhal stepped toward him and swung at him to push him farther away from his blade.

Dante crumbled to the ground in a heap as he squeezed his abdomen. The pain was agonizing, and he felt like he was going to pass out, but he held onto his consciousness. He could see Aliyah running toward him and grimaced as he grabbed his sword and started standing.

"Stay back!" Dante shouted to Aliyah. "I'll be okay, if you get too close, Damon will target you. I can't let that happen."

"I can heal you," Aliyah shouted back as she stopped in her tracks.

"I'm fine," Dante shouted back as he tried to shake the pain he was in. "Just focus on Damon."

Aliyah nodded and grabbed another arrow from her quiver. She was getting low and only had three shots left before she would be out, so she had to pick and choose her attacks wisely. She readied her bow and waited for the right time to strike.

Dante regained his footing and rushed back in to continue fighting. He knew he was outclassed, underpowered, and lacked experience, but his determination to avenge his friends far outweighed his desire for safety. He stepped back in and continued to attack where he could without hesitation.

Without his sword, Damon was less of a threat, but was still incredibly dangerous. Diabhal kept him on the defensive by pouring on attacks, but none landed. Dante tried to intervene where he could, but his attacks were still not breaking through the barrier. It seemed like Damon had all the time and energy in the world to keep fighting.

Aliyah watched Damon carefully, trying to study his movements and see if there were any exploitable weaknesses in his attacks, but the King seemed perfectly impenetrable. Her arm began to feel weak as she held her bow in place, waiting for the right time to strike. She quickly loosed her arrow the moment she saw it.

Damon managed to find an opening to attack and was about to slam his palm into Diabhal's chest. Aliyah knew she couldn't hit Damon, but also knew her arrows weren't translucent. She landed her shot right in front of his eye, disrupting his vision enough to force a mistake, and saved Diabhal from a surely devastating attack.

Dante saw the arrow and tried to follow it with a blasting swing toward his eyes, hoping to overwhelm the barrier, but it was blocked the same as before. Damon tried to grab Dante, but yet another arrow struck directly in front of his eyes and gave him enough room to avoid getting snagged.

Damon grew angry and yelled in frustration. Diabhal saw this as an opportunity to attack. He rapidly sliced his blade at Damon's neck, hoping to cleave his head from his shoulders. The King saw the attack coming and sprung a plan into action. He slammed his palm into Diabhal's wrist, snapping the bone with ease and separating his sword from his grasp.

Diabhal growled in pain as he watched Damon grab his blade out of the air and use it for himself. The King slammed an elbow into Diabhal's nose and spun to the side. Dante tried to step in and attack, but didn't see that Damon was actually targeting him.

Dante was defenseless as he felt the blade slam into his neck. He saw Diabhal tackle Damon the moment he was struck, but it didn't save him from the damage. The blade sliced across his body and flayed him open from neck to hip, ripping through clothes, skin, and muscle as the attack cut him down.

"So this is it," Dante thought to himself as he felt the attack tear him apart. "This is where my journey ends. I'm sorry, Faetu. I tried. I'm just not strong enough."

Dante's legs gave out from underneath him as he watched Damon slam his palm into Diabhal's back to knock him to the ground. The King stepped over his mentor and looked right at Dante. There was nothing he could do anymore except wait for the final blow that would kill him.

"Damnit," Dante thought, "I really thought we could win this time."

As Dante watched Damon draw back his blade, his vision began to blur. He felt like he was about to die already, meaning Damon was wasting his time coming for the finishing blow. His senses began to go numb, and his ears started to ring in a deafening tone. His vision was overtaken by a bright white light that consumed everything he looked at, and the light was painful to behold.

"Is this the gateway to heaven?" Dante wondered.

However, he suddenly felt something grab the back of his collar and start pulling him away. The stone beneath his body was abrasive as he was dragged across it, but his vision was returning. He could see Diabhal had grabbed Damon again, this time successfully tackling him to the ground, and that Aliyah was just above him.

"Aliyah?" Dante spoke softly.

A look of panic was on her face as she frantically stopped dragging him, placed her hands on Dante's chest, and whispered, "Please don't die, Dante. I can't lose you, too."

Aliyah poured everything she had through her body and surged it into Dante's. Her healing magic worked faster than it ever had before, and the massive gash on Dante's body began to pull itself back together. Dante was amazed at how well her magic was working and could feel the invigorating rush of energy flowing from her fingertips. He knew it must be exhausting, and his heart warmed as he saw what lengths she was going to go to save him.

"Stay with me, okay?" Aliyah said through a grimace.

A smile crept across Dante's face as he felt the pain in his chest start to vanish. The stinging sensation disappeared, and the rush of blood stopped. He saw Aliyah take a deep breath and smile at him as well.

"Thank you, Aliyah," Dante said.

"I couldn't have you dying on me, you're destined for greatness, remember?" Aliyah replied. "Now, let's finish this."

Dante jumped to his feet and helped Aliyah up afterward, saying, "Let's."

They turned their attention back toward Damon, but were stunned at what they saw. Diabhal was lying on the ground behind the King. His face appeared bloody, and he wasn't moving. Damon was facing them with his palm outward and had a sinister grin on his face.

"This is over," Damon muttered.

Gray-tinted energy quickly swirled down Damon's arm and blasted out of his palm, just as it did in their first battle. The attack ripped through the room almost faster than they could react, but Dante quickly shoved Aliyah out of the way of its path.

Aliyah panicked. She didn't want to see Dante die the same way Aslan did. She couldn't bear the thought of watching yet another friend being killed in front of her. In her desperation, she tried to use her powers in a way she never had before. Her energy gathered into the tips of her fingers, and she wanted to push Dante away, to protect him, but she didn't know how.

Each millisecond felt like an hour as she watched the magic beam inching toward Dante's head. No matter how hard she tried, she couldn't grab him, and she couldn't release her healing magic at a distance. The only thing she could do was watch as Dante would be inevitably ripped to shreds, just like Aslan was. She focused on the tip of the attack, almost wishing she could push it away.

As the beam was centimeters from making contact with Dante's ear, it seemed to make contact with something. A prismatic glow emanated from the point of impact and caused it to erupt violently, sending Dante tumbling to the side until he came to a crashing halt against the wall. Aliyah desperately scrambled to her feet as she ran over to him, but she was haunted by Damon's taunting laughter from behind.

"How many of your friends are willing to die for you?" Damon asked aloud. "Go, run to your corpse of a friend, I'll relish in your despair."

Aliyah didn't listen. She couldn't understand how, but she was sure she had done something to the attack. She needed to know if Dante was okay, or if she was losing her mind. She dropped down next to him and rolled him over onto his back and immediately began to sob.

"Dante," Aliyah said through tears as she hugged him.

"What did you do?" Dante asked, amazed that he was still alive.

"I don't know, it was like I made a force field for a brief moment. I can't explain it, my body just reacted," Aliyah struggled to elaborate.

"Well, that's twice now, I owe you my life," Dante muttered.

"Well, well," Damon announced as he looked at them. "I'll admit, I'm impressed. It won't save you, but you get to die knowing you're the first people I've killed that gave me the slightest of challenges." Damon held his palm out in front of him again as he muttered, "But how many times can you do that?"

Gray-tinted magic began to swirl down his arm once more, and neither of them was sure what to do. The distance between them and Damon was far too great to cover, and they would have to dodge multiple attacks if they wanted to try. Fleeing wasn't an option either, so Aliyah prepared herself to try to repeat the force field she used before.

The magic collected in Damon's palm and looked as though it was about to blast toward them when it suddenly vanished. They saw the look in Damon's eyes immediately widen before he looked down at his chest and saw the tip of his sword sticking out of his body. Diabhal's black flames wrapped around the edges of the blade and burned in his insides. Damon dropped his sword and reached for the blade in his body with trembling fingers. As he placed his hand on the weapon, Diabhal jerked it back out of him, and he collapsed to his knees.

"It is time, young Damon," Diabhal said with a sigh. "Monsters like us have no place here."

"Damn you.. Diabhal," Damon muttered as he looked at the blood flowing from where his heart should be.

"I will be joining you soon," Diabhal mumbled.

Damon could feel his life slipping away as a warm rush began to wash across his body. Blood slowly began to soak into his clothing, but with his heart destroyed, the bleeding wasn't as quick. Damon looked up one last time at Dante and Aliyah before he fell onto his face and stopped breathing. A loud caw of a crow echoed around the room as soon as Damon touched the soil. The King was dead.

Chapter 12

"I can't believe it," Aliyah said, nearly bursting into tears, "It's finally over."

"He's really dead," Dante said as he dropped his sword beside him. "We can finally be free."

Dante grabbed Aliyah and squeezed her with a tight hug. She wrapped her arms around him as well, and they embraced one another for a long time, without saying a word or moving an inch, just enjoying the warmth of each other's bodies. However, their moment of peace was abruptly interrupted.

"Pick up your sword," Diabhal said, still standing over Damon's body.

Dante let go of the hug and looked at Diabhal. He was bloody, holding Damon's sword in his off hand, and staring at them through his eyebrows.

"Why?" Dante asked.

"Pick up your sword," Diabhal demanded.

"What do you mean?" Dante asked, beginning to worry. "The battle is over. Why pick up my weapon?"

"We're not done here," Diabhal said as he rekindled the flames on his blade. "Now pick up your sword."

"I don't understand. What are you saying?" Dante asked. He thought, "This isn't good. If Diabhal attacks me, I'll be dead in a single blow. I can't fight, but I'm not fast enough to run, and neither is Aliyah. I can't even stay behind so she can get away, she won't get far enough. What the hells can I do?"

"I am a killer, and I will keep killing until I draw my final breath, or until there is no life left around for me to take," Diabhal explained. "I don't want to keep killing, I don't want to see any more faces in my dreams, but it's who I am."

"I thought you said you were putting all this to rest when Damon was killed?" Aliyah asked.

"I am, for good. You will kill me or die, it's your choice," Diabhal declared.

"If you want to die, then why are you holding onto a weapon?" Dante asked.

As he listened to Diabhal, panic began to grow in the pit of his stomach and he thought, "What is he doing? Why does he want to fight? Why doesn't he just walk away and live the rest of his life elsewhere. I have to do something, maybe talk him out of it? I can't fight him, he'll kill me in an instant, so I have to talk him down."

"Because a Ghost of War who doesn't die in battle is damned to continue fighting until the universe meets its end. So I must die fighting, and you'll have to do it. If you fail, I will search these lands for anyone strong enough to take me down," Diabhal elaborated. "Now, I am done explaining. For the final time, pick up your sword. You get no more warnings."

"Please, lis-," Dante tried to bargain, but he was cut short.

Diabhal grew tired of waiting. He painfully held his broken hand out and blasted a plume of erratic flames toward the two of them. Luckily for them, the fire was nowhere near as fast as Damon's attack, and they were able to slip away from its heat.

Dante grabbed his sword as he and Aliyah rolled to the side to avoid getting burned, but Diabhal quickly closed the distance. Dante threw his blade upward to deflect a downward strike, redirecting the burning sword to his side and allowing them to take another step back to create distance.

"Diabhal, listen, it doesn't have to be like this," Aliyah shouted.

"I'm done talking, fight or die," Diabhal growled as he lunged back toward them.

Diabhal jumped back in and swung his blade at Dante's throat. The attack was swift, but Aliyah quickly created a force field to protect Dante, saving him from the fatal blow. Dante tried to swipe his blade across Diabhal's chest, but his attack was easily avoided. Diabhal retaliated by slamming his sword downward toward Dante's skull.

Attack after attack, Diabhal threw, but Aliyah blocked each of them with her force fields. She was doing her best to keep up with Diabhal's pace, but was struggling to use her power as she had already pushed close to her limits. She was breathing heavily but was determined to keep Dante alive.

"How am I supposed to kill him?" Dante wondered in a panic. "He's bloody, broken, and fighting with the wrong arm.

Yet I still can't land a single attack. If I don't figure something out, we're going to die."

Dante tried to do everything he could, but nothing was working. Luckily for him, Aliyah was covering his back, or he would have long been dead. He swiped his sword at Diabhal's neck, but the attack was redirected, and he saw the prismatic shimmer as a sword slammed next to his ear. He tried to thrust his blade toward Diabhal's stomach, but the attack was parried, and he heard the sound of a sword slamming against a forcefield just behind his head.

Over and over again, Dante tried to attack, but landed nothing. Each time he swung his blade, it was dodged or parried, and he was forced to hear the sound of Aliyah's forcefield saving his life. This continued again and again until Diabhal grew frustrated.

In the midst of his anger, Diabhal began to incorporate his broken hand into his attack chain. He swung his sword, and when the attack was blocked, he would smash his fist into Dante. The punches hurt him almost as much as they hurt his opponent, but he fought like a demon hellbent on bringing death to those around him. Dante felt a thunderous punch smash into the side of his face, followed by the stomach-turning sound of bones crunching underneath the force of the blow. He stumbled to the side from the punch, and Diabhal started to attack even more relentlessly.

"What kind of man is this?" Dante thought as he felt a knee lift into his face. "He has no regard for his own well-being. Who fights like this?"

Dante stumbled backward from the knee he took and saw a prismatic flash as Diabhal's sword nearly sliced into his neck. A chill went down his spine as he looked into Diabhal's eyes. They seemed devoid of humanity, as if he were nothing more than a devil in human skin. To add to his worries, the force field that Aliyah blocked the attack with seemed to buckle under the force of the swing, meaning he was getting stronger, or she was growing weaker.

Diabhal watched Dante struggle to keep his footing as he tried to stay between him and Aliyah. He paused briefly before saying, "Twenty-seven. Twenty-seven times, you would have died now. Twenty-seven times, you needed someone else to save you. Twenty-seven times, you were unworthy of living. Tell me, how long do you plan to keep this up? How long will you put forth such a meager attempt at keeping your soul in your body? What more do you have to lose before you start fighting to the fullest of your potential?"

"I can't beat you, Diabhal," Dante said as he wiped blood from his face. He could feel a cut under his left eye and blood falling from his nose. "You're too fast and too strong."

"That is weakness speaking," Diabhal shouted as he lunged back toward Dante.

He continued his assault, only growing faster with each swing. Aliyah was beginning to struggle with his pace, and her energy was all but gone. Her vision was foggy already as she desperately tried to give Dante a chance of survival, but she feared she couldn't keep it up much longer.

Dante was in a daze as his offense nearly slowed to a halt. What were once failed swings were now replaced with hesitation. He tried his best to protect himself, but even if he ignored the bladed attacks, the kicks and punches were still too fast for him to keep up with. He started to get pummeled, punch after punch, breaking his body down a little at a time. First to the face, then to the stomach, each hit hurting worse than the last.

"Damnit," Dante scolded himself silently. "I have to do something. What can I do?"

He began to look for anything that might help swing the fight in his favor, even if it were a long shot. He could see the force fields were continuing to weaken, as Diabhal's blade started to swing close enough to open minor cuts on his body. He was running out of time when he finally had an idea.

As soon as Diabhal swung his arm, Dante dropped his blade, grabbed Diabhal's hand, and slammed a punch into his face. Dante felt a glimmer of hope stream through his mind as he finally landed a blow on this impossible foe. But Diabhal didn't miss a beat.

By now, his hand was a mangled mess. Nearly every bone in his hand and wrist was shattered, and it looked like he would never recover use of his hand again. Dante could feel the bones shifting beneath his grasp, but he didn't want to let go. As long as he held on, he would only need to dodge attacks from his sword. Diabhal knew this and reacted unexpectedly.

In the blink of an eye, Diabhal swung his blade at Dante to occupy Aliyah's forcefield, planted his foot into Dante's chest, and yanked on his own arm to rip his limb apart at the wrist. The skin on his wrist tore in a bloody mess, and exposed bones protruded from the end of his arm, but his expression never changed. It was like he couldn't feel the agonizing pain he must have been in.

Dante was dumbfounded at what he witnessed. The idea of someone tearing their own hand off never crossed his mind, even from an enemy like this. He looked down at the severed hand and dropped it in disgust. As soon as he turned his attention back to Diabhal, he saw the man using the exposed bone at the end of his arm as a spear.

Diabhal drove his bone toward Dante's chest, slamming into the forcefield yet again, but this time it didn't hold. The forcefield diverted the attack slightly, but it shattered almost immediately, and Dante felt the bone stab into his shoulder. He screamed out in pain as the jagged bone tore through his flesh and into his shoulder. Digging as deep as it could before he ran out of exposed bone.

Dante's arms fell limp. His will to fight was gone, as he knew he couldn't compete with a madman drunk on bloodlust. He grimaced in agony as Diabhal lifted him by the piercing wound and suspended him in the air.

"It would seem your luck has run out, Dante. I was hoping you would rise to the occasion. It seems I was wrong," Diabhal said with a genuinely saddened look in his eye.

"Go to hell," Dante said before he spat blood into Diabhal's face.

"I hope I meet you there soon," Diabhal responded as he raised his sword.

Before he could slice open Dante's throat, an arrow was buried in his shoulder, forcing him to stop the attack. Diabhal saw Aliyah standing just behind Dante, breathing heavily, and now she was out of ammunition. He lifted Dante, kicked him in the chest with monumental force, and sent him flying toward her.

Aliyah reached out and grabbed Dante, slowing his momentum as she caught him in her arms. Dante was surprised she had the energy to catch him, but had no time to process anything. He watched Diabhal's blade pass over his head. He followed the attack with his eyes as it passed over him entirely and tore through Aliyah's throat. He lunged at her directly after he kicked Dante, using his body as camouflage to mask his approach. She never saw the attack coming. Both Aliyah and Dante fell to the ground immediately.

Dante felt a surge of panicked adrenaline wash over him as he hurried to his knees and grabbed Aliyah. He held his hand over the massive gash on her neck as he started to hyperventilate. His heart felt like it was beating faster than humanly possible, and he could feel his blood flowing through his veins at an alarming rate.

"No, no, no, no," Dante whispered. "Please, no. Aliyah, please don't go."

Fear sat in her eyes as she repeatedly failed to take in a breath. Each time she tried, blood flowed into her lungs, and she started to drown. She wanted to heal herself, but she had no energy left. She spent every ounce she had protecting Dante and had no options left. In her final moments, she knew she was going to die, and there was nothing she could do to stop it. Dante tried desperately to apply pressure to the wound, but he had no medical knowledge and didn't know what to do.

Dante stared into Aliyah's eyes as she looked back into his. He could see the panic and fear in her eyes, and it tore at his psyche. He felt like his very being was about to collapse as he desperately searched every corner of his memory for anything that could help. But, as he hopelessly tried to think of something, her arms fell to her side. She died in his arms, and he felt frozen. His mind felt like it was fractured, and he didn't know what to do. His skin felt like a raging inferno, and he couldn't take in a breath. Despite his heart beating uncontrollably fast, no air would enter his lungs. He felt like he was going to puke, and his vision began to blur. To add to his woes, he felt a thunderous knee smash into his face that knocked him backward.

Diabhal slammed his exposed bone into Dante again, piercing his abdomen, and lifted him from the ground before saying, "You get no time to mourn in battle." Then he blasted him with a headbutt and kicked him again to send him flying through the air toward a wall on the opposite side of the room.

Time felt motionless as Dante soared through the air and thought, "Why? Why am I the only one alive? Aliyah was always helping people, but the one time she needed saving, I was pathetically incapable. Kinomaru gave his life to protect me. Faetu gave his life fighting harder than I ever did. Even Aslan gave his life to protect Aliyah.

All of these people are stronger than I am. So why am I the only one who lived? Why did all of these people die instead of me? What kind of cruel fate have I been given? Why am I forced to watch everyone die, to still die in the end? I didn't even get to tell her how I felt, and she looked so scared. I hate this, I hate this so much it hurts."

The blood flowing through his veins began to feel like gasoline as it burned at his insides. His body felt like it was overheating, and he could feel his consciousness slipping away.

"Is this what dying feels like?" he wondered. "Is this what everyone else felt? Am I even worthy to join them in the heavens? Or am I damned to walk the hells like the weakling I am? I can already feel the flames."

His body felt like it was about to explode into an inferno just before he slammed into the wall. He bounced off the stone and fell to the ground. Diabhal stared at Dante as his body fell to the ground with a thud, and he trembled in place. Dante was sure that was it for him, but for some reason, he didn't feel the pain. In fact, he felt better than he did before. He couldn't explain it, but it felt like the heat was somehow helping him.

"What is going on?" Dante thought as he looked down at his hands.

The scrapes and cuts were gone, healed entirely. His body didn't ache, the stab wounds were numb, and his limbs felt loose. He felt like his stamina was nonexistent yet unlimited at the same time.

"Is my body dying? Am I already dead?" Dante pondered. "I don't understand what is happening."

Diabhal rushed over and tried to kick Dante in the face, but he was able to block the attack and jump up to his feet. He was confused as to how he saw the attack coming, but didn't have enough time to dwell on it, as Diabhal continued his chain of attacks.

Dante swayed back to avoid a swipe of a sword, leaned to the side to avoid another stab of Diabhal's bone, lifted his leg to deflect a kick, and then finally blasted Diabhal in the face with a hard punch that forced him to back away.

Diabhal was surprised to see Dante suddenly gain so much power, but that surprise was met with excitement instead of fear. He grinned widely with a mouth full of blood.

"That's it, Dante," Diabhal shouted with glee. "It looks like you have more power than I thought."

Dante didn't say anything, he just stared through his eyebrows as he tried to think of what to do. But even his vision felt different. He could see his sword across the room, near Aliyah's body, and knew he had to get it if he wanted to live. He wasn't sure what was happening to him, so he didn't want to waste any time.

Diabhal waited for a moment as he tried to predict what Dante would do next, but as he stared into his eyes, he noticed something different. Dante's eyes were ocean blue, but now they had a yellow slit that ran through the center of his irises. He intensified the heat on his blade and charged in again.

Dante surprised him by lunging in to meet him halfway and blasting him in the face with a hard punch. Diabhal rolled with the hit and lifted a powerful knee into Dante's ribs, crunching one of them under the pressure. He tried to follow up the attack by slamming his sword into Dante's neck, but his attack was off target, and he only grazed his blade across Dante's shoulder.

Even after the burning pain of the attack, Dante pressed through and pushed his hand away to mitigate the damage. He followed that by spinning halfway around and putting his legs behind Diabhal's. He shoved Diabhal's upper body away while holding a leg behind his, tripping him to the ground and giving a second to create distance.

Diabhal landed hard on his back and rolled to his feet. At first, he didn't see Dante, but after a quick scan, he found him standing next to Aliyah with his sword in hand.

"You are going to die like the devil you are," Dante muttered as his sword began to emanate a yellowish glow. "You will pay in blood for what you've taken from me."

"Good," Diabhal responded with a crazed look in his eye.

The two dashed toward one another into the center of the room, and their blades collided. Black flames and plumes of yellow energy burst out in every direction, and Dante matched Diabhal's speed blow for blow. He wasn't sure how, but he could see things he hadn't before. Time seemed to move a little slower, and matching Diabhal's incredible speed wasn't nearly as difficult. However, he was still only able to match him, and landing a solid blow proved to be difficult.

As they tried desperately to cut one another down, they each left themselves open for small attacks. They began to chip away at one another, little by little, but barely doing more than breaking open skin. The more Dante tried to land an attack, the more he started to suffer more wounds. The black flames that lined Diabhal's sword were hotter than anything he had ever felt and caused pain far deeper than the cut itself. On top of that, he felt like Diabhal was somehow getting even faster, as if the thrill of death fueled his strength.

Diabhal swiped his blade toward Dante's skull, knowing he would duck underneath, and lifted a powerful knee into his face. Dante was rattled from the attack but managed to jump back and avoid an attack that would have severed his body in half. Even after jumping out of the way, the tip of Diabhal's sword still sliced across his abdomen, cutting him open slightly and adding yet another bleeding wound.

"If I take any more damage, I'm going to bleed out," Dante thought. "I have to do something, and fast. This fire in my veins scares me, and it feels like my heart is going to beat out of my chest, but I think I could use it. I just need to make sure the attack will land, otherwise I'm dead."

Diabhal stepped toward him again to close the distance and continued his relentless onslaught of attacks, except this time, Dante was entirely focused on defense as he figured out a way to end the fight. He blocked, dodged, and evaded all attacks that came his way until the answer came to him.

"Watch the shoulders," Dante remembered.

He stared intently at Diabhal, studying his body, paying close attention to any shift in his shoulders. That's when he saw his opening. Diabhal's shoulder began to shift slightly, giving a tell of where his next attack would come from, and Dante capitalized. He prepared himself to counter and already knew how he would strike next.

As soon as the attack came, Dante lifted his blade upward to force Diabhal's sword up and away from his body, then Dante quickly followed the momentum and turned his blade to slam it into Diabhal's chest. The churning blood in his veins was like lava as he focused all of his energy into his sword. The yellow light that ran along his blade began to glow brighter and brighter within a second, and Dante screamed at the top of his lungs as he slammed the edge of his blade into Diabhal's body.

The ground shook as his sword made contact, and an explosion of power erupted from the blade. A wave of force blasted out of the blade that was so powerful it tore up the ground in its path until it hit the wall on the opposite side of the room. The wall immediately crumbled to rubble, blowing a hole big enough for a dragon to fit through and sending massive stones tumbling down to the ground below.

Dante stood in front of Diabhal, breathing heavily, as he watched the flames on his sword vanish before he dropped the weapon to the ground. Diabhal's expression was one of joy as he looked Dante in the eyes and felt his body begin to slide apart. Diabhal fell to the ground in two pieces, quickly bleeding out and meeting the end he so desperately sought.

Chapter 13

Dante stood over Diabhal's body as he tried to catch his breath. He felt the air flow into his lungs and cool his blood as he started to calm, and the weight of everything that had just happened began to process in his mind. He lifted his blade and used the broad side of the weapon as a mirror to look at his own face. He barely recognized what he was looking at. His eyes looked like they belonged to someone else.

"Is this a result of that power? Is that my power?" Dante wondered. "Where did it come from? And why couldn't I use it sooner? Why did everyone I know have to die before I could finally be useful?"

As he stood, lost in thought, he began to hear footsteps on the stairs outside the door. He turned to face the entrance when the door burst open and dozens of guards stopped in their tracks. What they witnessed was stunning: Dante standing above the bodies of not only their King but also Diabhal, whom they knew to be just as strong as Damon. The destruction and devastation in the room was shocking, and they weren't sure what to do.

One of the guards shouted as he started running toward Dante, "How dare you harm King Damon!"

He ran toward Dante with his sword high, ready to strike, but didn't get the chance. Dante moved incredibly quickly and swiped the tip of his blade across the man's neck before he could even react, spilling his blood as he fell to his knees and hopelessly tried to hold onto the wound.

A second man was rushing in behind the first, but he fared no better. After Dante killed the first, he seemed to move five feet in the blink of an eye and grabbed the man by the throat. He lifted him off the ground and closed his hand around his neck until he ripped the front half of his neck to shreds. He dropped the second man on the ground to bleed out and die as he stared at the rest of the guards.

"Do any more of you wish to die today?" Dante asked menacingly.

The remaining guards looked around at one another, waiting for someone else to make the first move, but no one did. They knew they stood no chance against anyone who could kill Damon, and one by one they started to kneel. Dante watched them in with a confused look as he tried to understand what was happening, when it suddenly clicked. The Kingdom is run by the strongest, and he was the last one standing.

"We await your orders, sire," one of the guards shouted as he stared at the ground by his feet.

"Where is Kinomaru?" Dante asked.

"Do you mean the titan we faced on the bridge, sire?" a guard asked.

"Yes," Dante answered.

"He has perished, sire," he answered with a shaky voice, fearing for his life.

"How?" Dante asked again.

"We don't know. He just fell down and stopped moving. He killed over a hundred of us before he did, sire," another guard responded.

"I see," Dante muttered. "What will you do now?"

"As we said, we await your orders, sire," the guard answered.

"Why?" Dante asked, still defensive about getting attacked.

"Because only the strongest of us can lead this nation, the King of the Devalon Empire may only be the strongest of its people. Because you defeated King Damon, you are the strongest. You are the King, sire," a guard explained.

"King, huh?" Dante muttered again.

He thought about it for a long time, standing in silence as the guards knelt before him, "I never considered this as a possibility. This was Faetu's dream, not mine. But if I were King, I *could* change things. Yeah, I could fix this Kingdom and save its people. I could see this through to the end." He spoke out to the guards, "Tell me, where are all the soldiers?"

"They are all awaiting the orders of the King, standing prepared to assault Blackhold. What do you wish them to do, sire?" a guard asked.

"Tell them to stand down," Dante ordered.

"Excuse me, sire?" the guard asked for clarity.

"This Kingdom's days of conquest and destruction are over. We will no longer spread fear and foster hate. Anyone who raises a blade to harm an innocent life will answer to me. I will personally cut down anyone who tries to embody the monster Damon was. He was a demon who ruined lives, and anyone like him has no place here," Dante preached. "Spread the word that a new King has taken over, one that will rebuild this Kingdom from the ground up and regain the trust of its people. We will build a Kingdom that loves and protects its people at all costs. If we ever raise our blades, it will be in service to our people, and never against them. Now go, let everyone know, and find me in Dawnberry when you're finished."

"Yes, sire," the guards said in unison as they quickly stood and shuffled out of the room, leaving Dante there with the corpses of friends and foes alike.

Dante waited for them to leave before he dropped his sword by his side. He put on a front to intimidate the guards, but he was falling apart on the inside. He shambled over to Aliyah's body, fell to his knees, and slowly reached down to grab her and pull her close. His lip quivered and tears welled up in his eyes as he buried his face into her shoulder. The pain of grief and loss started to settle in as his adrenaline wound down.

"I'm so sorry, Aliyah," Dante said as he sobbed. "I'm sorry I couldn't save you. I'm sorry I wasn't strong enough when you needed me most. If I could trade you places right now, I would in an instant. I hope you find Faetu in the heavens and get a second chance at the life you couldn't have here.

I love you, Aliyah. I have loved you since we were kids, and I regret never telling you how I feel. I knew I could never measure up to Faetu, but I always dreamed I could earn your love one day. I pray you find peace and happiness in the heavens, Aliyah."

Dante sat there for a long time, holding the body of the woman he loved, struggling to let go. He stayed there until the sun started to rise, fighting through watery eyes, processing his emotions, and struggling to comprehend the outcome of the fight. His mind was fractured. Dealing with so much loss took its toll on him, and he didn't feel like the same man he was before they started this journey. He was stronger, faster, and more experienced, but alone.

Eventually, after hours of grieving, Dante was finally ready to stand. His legs had gone numb hours before, but he didn't care. The thought of letting go was excruciating, and he didn't want to accept his reality. He knew even more grief awaited him outside of the keep, as he would undoubtedly have to find the body of yet another one of his closest friends. His pain was immeasurable, and he couldn't come to terms with suffering so much loss in victory.

He slowly released his tight hug on Aliyah and gently rested her back on the floor. He immediately burst into tears as he looked at her face. The fear she had when she died still sat in her eyes, and it ripped him apart.

"I'm so sorry," Dante muttered over and over, not sure what else to say, but feeling solely responsible for everything that happened.

With no one to comfort him, Dante painstakingly walked away from Aliyah and out of the keep. He wasn't sure where, but he wanted to find somewhere to bury his friends. He holstered his sword before leaving the keep. He didn't care if one of the guards was ready to ambush him. By this time, he wanted to die too. It would mean the pain of loss would go away, but no one remained in the castle at all.

He sauntered his way down the stairs, out the door, and onto the bridge. He immediately saw Kinomaru's body only a few feet from the door, and a sea of corpses past him. A hundred men lay dead, suffering grievous wounds at the hand of Kinomaru's wrath. Dante fell to his knees next to his friend and looked at his face, noticing that there wasn't a single wound on his body.

"I hope you found peace, Kino... Kyojin," Dante mumbled. "I'm so sorry I was too blind to see your struggles, but I owe you my life. I pray I get to thank you in the afterlife one day."

His grief had consumed his soul to the point of numbness. Everyone he cared about was gone. He was left alone to navigate the rest of his life without a shoulder to lean on or friends to confide in. The hollow feeling of loneliness was all that remained.

Dante stood back up and continued to walk out of the castle. His mind wandered as it struggled to survive amid his emotions. His internal battle was devastating, but he felt disconnected from it as numbness covered the pain. Before he knew it, he found himself outside the castle, and he looked up the hill from where he was standing and knew where he wanted to bury his friends.

Dante spent the entire day digging two graves. One for Aliyah and one for Kinomaru. It took him a long time, but eventually the job was done, and he started to move their bodies out of the castle. After some effort, he managed to get

Kinomaru and Aliyah into the graves he had dug and began filling the holes with soil. Little by little, he shoveled dirt until the bodies of the last friends he had were covered and buried.

After he finished, he was covered in sweat, and his body felt like it was going to give out on him as he stood over them and said, "I owe each of you my life. Just as Faetu and Aslan did, you gave your lives protecting others. I will never measure up to you, but I hope to make all of you proud one day. I will carry you with me in my heart until I am granted the opportunity to walk by your side once more. I only hope you can forgive me for my failures when I do. I will miss all of you so much, and I would gladly trade places with you in an instant if I could. Please, wait for me, I don't want to be alone in death as well."

After he finished, he turned away and started walking north toward Dawnberry. He had no intention of burying the bodies of Damon, Diabhal, or any of the guards. He was just going to let them rot where they lay, in an unmarked castle of corpses, a memorial of the disgusting reality of how low humanity could stoop.

Dante did not rush his trip back to Dawnberry. He was afraid to face Hendrickson and tell him what happened. Even if he were the new King, he didn't feel any different. He still felt like the weak little boy getting his face shoved into the dirt. The only difference was that no one was left strong enough to put him in that position. With his new power, Dante was the strongest person in the Kingdom, and he vowed to use that strength to protect.

It took days, but Dante finally arrived in Dawnberry. Some of the villagers gave him an odd look as he walked through the streets. He was bloody, bruised, and his clothes were shredded. None of them had any idea what he had suffered through; they only saw the disheveled mess he was.

After some time, he finally saw the guard house ahead of him and slowly made his way through the door. Hendrickson was sitting behind the desk when he walked in and immediately jumped up to greet him.

"Oh my heavens," Hendrickson said as he looked at Dante, "You look like you've been tortured. How bad are your injuries? Where are you hurt? What's wrong with your eyes?"

Hendrickson rushed over to him and began to look him over for any wounds, but aside from some bruising, Dante was unharmed. Despite his age, Hendrickson still viewed Dante as a child, and he was deeply worried about his health. Once he made sure Dante didn't need medical attention, he raised his head and looked toward the door, but no one else was with him.

Dante began to shake as tears welled up in his eyes before saying, "They're all gone. I'm the only one left. I'm so sorry."

Hendrickson was also fighting back tears as he closed his eyes and slowly shook his head. He stepped back and reached for somewhere to sit down as he took a slow breath.

"I had a feeling I shouldn't have let you all go," Hendrickson said quietly. "I knew you all were headed for trouble, but I can't keep you on a leash. I've failed all of you. Where did you go?"

"We went to kill the King," Dante answered.

"I figured as much," Hendrickson sighed. "I only hope your actions haven't doomed us all."

"Everyone here is safe," Dante answered.

"How can you be so sure?" Hendrickson asked.

"Because Damon is dead," Dante replied.

Hendrickson leaned forward in his seat with a bewildered look as he said, "What?!?"

"Yes, but it came at far too great a cost," Dante answered. "If I could take it back, I would."

"I can't believe he's actually dead," Hendrickson muttered as he ran his fingers through his hair in disbelief. "I wonder who will assume the role."

"I am," Dante said quietly.

"Huh?" Hendrickson asked for clarity.

"I am the new King," Dante responded.

"What do you mean? How?" Hendrickson interrogated.

"Because I was the only one left," Dante said as he stared into nothingness, the pain of his loneliness rushing to the forefront of his mind.

"I can't believe what I'm hearing," Hendrickson stated. "I would say this is cause for celebration, but my heart is too heavy to cheer."

"I don't want to celebrate. I want everyone here to recognize Faetu, Aslan, Kinomaru, and Aliyah for the heroes they are. I want the people of Dawnberry to feel proud of their sacrifice and celebrate their greatness. Forget about me," Dante instructed.

"Okay," Hendrickson agreed. "I will be sure to commission memorials in their honor. But what will you do?"

"I don't know," Dante answered. I don't know what to do. I've never been a leader, and I don't know how to run a Kingdom. But knights will be coming here soon, seeking guidance and direction. I am nothing more than a foolish boy wearing a King's persona."

"I can try to help," Hendrickson offered. "I have been leading Dawnberry for decades. It's no Kingdom, but I may be able to give you some tips to get you through the growing pains."

Dante nearly burst into tears as Hendrickson spoke. He replied, "I would like that."

Hendrickson spent the next month trying his best to teach Dante everything he knew about leadership. Dante soaked in the information like a sponge and clung to his wisdom. But after the month passed, the knights arrived, and Dante had no choice but to take the lead himself.

Over the next year, Dante learned a lot about the Kingdom and the plans Damon had in place. He discovered that Damon planned to hunt down Kavronax the Vile and harness his strength, to spread the Kingdom farther south than Blackhold, and eventually push northward until he reached the Onyx Mountains. Damon was on the verge of creating the largest Kingdom in history, and no one could have stopped him.

As he learned more and more, Dante realized just how many lives were saved. He burned the plans Damon had in front of the generals of the armies and warned them against any form of conquest. He personally warned all his subordinates that defying this order would be punishable by death. He would not tolerate needless violence.

Many of his army's members left; some retired to live peaceful lives, some began new lives as mercenaries, and some even joined foreign armies in hopes of battling against Dante's rule. Everyone didn't immediately accept him, as some in the Kingdom agreed with Damon's bloodlust. But Dante was unbothered by the opinions of violent men and women.

He spent his time traveling from village to village, meeting with the people and expressing his plans for the future. He listened to their problems and tried his best to come up with solutions to issues he could address at his level. As with any leader, some people weren't happy with his choices, but most of the people were pleased to see the Kingdom moving in a direction that could not only provide prosperity but also safety.

He insisted they speak freely of their opinions and not to fear backlash for speaking their minds. He believed it was the people's right to help guide the direction of the Kingdom, and insisted that each village elect a leader who would meet with him yearly to raise concerns or issues, providing everyone with a voice in the throne room.

By the time his first year as King had passed, the military shifted from conquest to defence, and the borders of the Kingdom became more rigid instead of expanding. There were small attempts by outside forces to push the boundaries of the Kingdom and test his resolve, but they were surprised to find that such a kind King could react with such incredible violence. Even though he cared for his people, Dante swiftly cut down any outsiders who tried to harm them and defended his land with extreme aggression. Thousands of bodies would lie unclaimed at the borders of his territory, and he had no intention of changing.

Because of this, Dante found it difficult to strike up political relationships with bordering Kingdoms. The elves of Estaluna looked at him like a murderer because he slaughtered a band of their people. The people he killed were the assassins from the Hallowed Shroud, but in the eyes of the public, that organization was nothing more than a myth.

An alliance called the Knight's Court, which was housed to the south in Blackhold, shunned him for refusing to help them hunt and kill Kavronax the Vile. Dante was still trying to repair his own Kingdom, and didn't trust the army enough to send it to the south to assist. This led to a poor image in the eyes of the people of Blackhold.

Despite this, Dante managed to turn the Kingdom around in his first year, and each of his villages was already beginning to prosper. The majority of the citizens were in favor of their new King, and he was pleased to see the happiness on the faces of those around him. It warmed his heart to see Faetu's dream come to fruition.

On the anniversary of his becoming King, he traveled away from everything and everyone, just to be alone. He remembered the mountain he had seen when they were first approaching the castle, and found a specific spot where he could see it more clearly. The sun shone, illuminating the beautiful green grass that covered a hillside. He found a shady spot underneath a great maple tree and sat down at the edge of the hilltop, just before it sloped downward to a large plane filled with wildflowers.

"It's been a long time, Faetu," Dante said as he looked next to him.

Dante stared out toward the mountain and admired the waterfall that sprang forth from its center. The scene was picturesque and beautiful, like something a painter would put on display for all to see. He looked around him, and his heart warmed; they were just like he remembered them.

To his left was Faetu, sitting back on his arms with a smile on his face. Kinomaru was leaning against a large boulder beneath the maple tree, and Aslan was relaxing back in one of the branches above him. Aliyah was to his right and greeted him with the most soul-warming smile he had ever seen. Dante smiled back before he looked toward the tree at two grave markers about ten feet from the trunk, then back out at the waterfall.

"Faetu, I understand everything now," Dante said quietly. "You were right all along."

THE END

If you enjoyed the story, I would love to hear your thoughts! Reviews are the best way to help small authors like me spread the word about our stories!

Supplementary Information

Idrasi People

A race of large humans that harness incredibly powerful magic. They speak incantations that bolster their strength and resilience, making them nearly unstoppable. The incantations are said to have borrowed power from the god Dagda, and some believe the Idrasi are descendants of Dagda himself. However, the Idrasi are peaceful people, and want nothing more than to live in harmony with the world around them. But a desperate warlord named Razghul was determined to take their land and power by force. He launched wave after wave of attacks on them, but each battle was met with defeat. Unable to cope with his failure, he sacrificed everything to curse the Idrasi and doom them to extinction. The curse cost the soul of the warlord as well as what remained of his empire in a final attempt to end the Idrasi and wipe them from existence along with them. The source of the curse is unknown, but any Idrasi who speaks a word shall die before the sun rises the following day.

The Devalon Empire

The Kingdom run by King Dante. This Kingdom is an old Kingdom that stretches between Blackhold and Dawnberry. The Kingdom has had its ups and downs, but the current King is considered to be one of their better leaders. King Dante is generous for the most part, and cares about the safety of his borders, but he isn't afraid to carve a path in blood if it benefits his people.

Ghosts of War

The Ghosts of War were a feared and dangerous organization that ended tens of thousands of lives in their time. Their general worked closely with the King and acted as both his front line against opposing armies as well as his arrow that struck from the shadows. They were treated like a myth because no one who faced them lived to tell the tale. The Ghosts of War were the most dangerous military organization in all the surrounding regions, and the King used them wherever he saw fit. Even their home, Stormhelm Castle, was not located on any maps, and no one but outside of their army knew where it was except for the King.

Hallowed Shroud

An organization of high elf assassins that operate unknown to the common people, but as an asset to the government in the city they hail from. This organization conscripts children at a young age and inducts them into their ranks, molding them and training them to become assassins by nature. They are brainwashed to follow commands and think only of the mission. Assassins of the Hallowed Shroud are some of the most efficient and undetectable killing machines, even going as far as conducting long term undercover operations. Attempting to leave the ranks is an offense punishable by death.

Knight's Court

The Knight's Court is an organization of lords and merchants that have banded together to help people however they can. They hire adventurers to stamp out potential criminals, and even investigate more severe organizations.

They house themselves in cities, with their primary stronghold being located in Blackhold.

Kinomaru's Incantation

Kinomaru spoke a chant before he held off hundreds of guards on the bridge to the keep. He spoke these lines in his native tongue, but this is the english translation: "May my body become the shield that protects, my hammer the spear that fends off evil, and my eyes the lenses through which no trickery can remain hidden. Under the weight of my hammer shall those who seek destruction find their final resting place. May Dagda's harp play a melody that turns my blood into fuel that burns the flames of my soul and ignites the wrath of my people. On this day, I fight for the grace of Dagda."

The Pantheon of Gods

Aether - The God of light and the rising of the sun. People of divine spirit pay their respects to this god. The rising sun is attributed to the work of Aether, and people pray to him for new beginnings and bountiful sunlight.

Anansi - The Goddess of lies. The followers of Anansi find joy in deception and trickery. Thieves, deceivers, and political figures all pay their respects to Anansi, typically in private, and use her blessing to get away with nefarious plots. It is said that those who appease Anansi will be granted great power in return

Apollo - The God of the sun and healing. Apollo is credited for the light of the sun, and the healing energy of its rays. People who follow Apollo are lovers of the healing light of the sun and try to spread his grace far and wide.

Ceridwen - The Goddess of health and rebirth. People pray to this goddess for health and a chance at a new life. On rare occasions, she is known to grant people life anew, though this is typically accepted as legend more than fact..

Cernunnos - The God of nature. Lovers of nature, especially druidic circles, worship Cernunnos as he holds domain over nature and the cycle of life. He is known to hold balance as a core principal, and his followers strive to keep balance everywhere they go.

Dagda - The God of peace and destruction. Dagda is both the god of peace and hailed as a god of war. His followers pray to him for peace, but also to grant them the strength to stamp out those who would seek violence against them. He is the main god of the Idrasi people, as they are believed to be his direct descendants.

Danu - The Goddess of earth, land, and fertility. She is one of the lesser deities in the pantheon, but is known to spread wisdom to those who worship her. Followers of Danu take her teachings and use them to benefit the entirety of life around them.

Dian Cecht - The God of healing. He is another of the lesser deities, but his feats of healing magic and abilities are known throughout the land. Followers of Dian Cecht are devout in their desire to help others, and some are believed to be direct descendants of his, with the blood of a god running through their veins.

Fjordr - The God of fortune and good luck. People pray to this god for good fortune and plentiful sales. It is said a blessing from Fjordr will make even the unluckiest of men rich.

Forseti - The God of justice. Followers of Forseti are typically people who hold Justice over their own personal opinions. No matter how they feel, right and wrong are written in stone, and the law should dictate the fate of another.

Surtr - The God of renewal. Followers of Surtr are as chaotic as they are predictable. Believers in the rebirth of the world, Surtr's disciples want nothing more than to empower their god so he can walk the mortal plane and burn everything to ash so that the world can be reborn, free from the sins of mortals.

Tyr - The God of war. Revered by the strong, Tyr is the deity that receives the most recognition from those destined for battle. His followers believe that the strong control the weak, and that appeasing him will grant them fortune in the battles of their future.

Ugmamu - The God of dragons and the first dragon to ever exist. All dragons owe their lives and bloodline to this God. He is not worshipped like other Gods and Goddesses, instead, he is viewed as the father of dragons and the keeper of their souls. Every dragon that is granted life is believed to be hand placed by Ugmamu himself.

The Realms

Paxanthus - A world that sits on the outskirts of the realms. Travel to and from Paxanthus is incredibly rare, so much so that the vast majority of the realms are unaware of its existence. The people of Paxanthus are a powerful people, most of whom can harness incredible magic power to some degree, and they represent their Territories with pride. Earth, Air, Fire, Water, Light, and Dark are the six elements that make up the entirety of Paxanthian power. The Overseer, who is the only person on Paxanthus who can wield every element, sits at the pinnacle of its power structure.

Paxanthus has a culture rich with history, mostly of violence and bloodshed, but also of triumph and overcoming impossible odds. From battling a dragon of foretold doom, fighting to thwart an evil from a foreign realm, to struggling tooth and nail to combat the evil Paxanthus itself created. The people are steadfast, hearty, and resilient, not easily defeated by anything that wishes to bring them down.

Altomir - A realm that is overrun by bandit factions that control the entire population. The bandit factions are numerous, and are regularly changing with time, but always a threat that sits loosely around the neck of anyone wasting a peaceful life. Those born with any sort of magic potential are almost guaranteed to be recruited into a bandit faction and used as a weapon to serve the faction they belong to. Those who try to stand against the criminals that run the world are swiftly dealt with and used as an example to keep the rest of the population in line. Evil triumphs on Altomir, and it will take a miracle of incredible proportions to change anything.

Tahlav - Is a vast and diverse world, filled with an incredible array of races and cultures that change with time and fill every crevice of the landscape. Tahlav's history is incredibly rich, with Kingdoms coming and going, along with the rulers that lead them. There are elves that live a thousand years and dragonkin that live a hundred. Dwarves, elves, humans, and more populate this world, leading to legends and adventures far and wide.